THREE ON ONE

Skye Fargo saw what was happening, and didn't like what he saw. Three U.S. troopers and one Cheyenne girl. The girl was on her back. One trooper held her arms down above her head. The second trooper held her legs apart. The third, their sergeant, knelt above her.

"That'll be enough, Sergeant," Fargo said.

"Keep riding and fast, mister," the sergeant snarled. "This is army business."

Fargo's mouth tightened. He saw from the flush on the soldiers' faces and the lust in their eyes that they weren't going to listen to words.

But the Trailsman had something else to do his talking. His fists. His knife. And his gun. . . .

THE
TRAILSMAN

130

MONTANA
FIRE SMOKE

by

Jon Sharpe

A SIGNET BOOK

SIGNET
Published by the Penguin Group
Penguin Books USA Inc., 375 Hudson Street,
New York, New York 10014, U.S.A.
Penguin Books Ltd, 27 Wrights Lane,
London W8 5TZ, England
Penguin Books Australia Ltd, Ringwood,
Victoria, Australia
Penguin Books Canada Ltd, 10 Alcorn Avenue,
Toronto, Ontario, Canada M4V 3B2
Penguin Books (N.Z.) Ltd, 182-190 Wairau Road,
Auckland 10, New Zealand

Penguin Books Ltd, Registered Offices:
Harmondsworth, Middlesex, England

First published by Signet, an imprint of New American Library,
a division of Penguin Books USA Inc.

First Printing, October, 1992
10 9 8 7 6 5 4 3 2 1

 REGISTERED TRADEMARK—MARCA REGISTRADA

The first chapter of this book previously appeared in *The Silver Maria*,
the one hundred and twenty-ninth volume in this series.

Printed in the United States of America

The Trailsman

Beginnings . . . they bend the tree and they
mark the man. Skye Fargo was born when he
was eighteen. Terror was his midwife, vengeance
his first cry. Killing spawned Skye Fargo, ruthless, cold-blooded murder. Out of the acrid
smoke of gunpowder still hanging in the air, he
rose, cried out a promise never forgotten.

The Trailsman they began to call him all across
the West: searcher, scout, hunter, the man who
could see where others only looked, his skills for
hire but not his soul, the man who lived each
day to the fullest, yet trailed each tomorrow.
Skye Fargo, the Trailsman, the seeker who could
take the wildness of a land and the wanting of a
woman and make them his own.

*1860, the Montana Territory
north of Medicine Rocks,
a tinderbox waiting to ignite . . .*

1

Trouble. Just over the top of the ridge.

The ears told him. Not his ears, the tall, black-furred ears of the magnificent Ovaro he rode. They were flicking forward, then back, turning sideways then forward again. Those ears always told him when there was something even his own wild-creature hearing hadn't picked up. Skye Fargo moved the horse forward and carefully crested the ridge to look down a short slope thick with fescue grasses and wiry brush. He instantly saw the figure near the bottom; it was a girl, half running and half falling down the other side of the slope.

Indian, he thought when he saw the jet-black hair and slender shape under the deerskin dress. Northern Cheyenne. Every tribe had its distinctive way of cutting women's garments, and this one had the rounded contours of the upper sleeves and the straight line across the garment that marked the Cheyenne style. Skye Fargo's lake-blue eyes narrowed as he sat motionless atop the Ovaro with its black fore- and hindquarters and pure white midsection gleaming in the afternoon sun. The young woman was plainly running in fear, and he was wondering why when the three U.S. Cavalry troopers rode into sight on their dark bay army mounts. One immediately sent his horse down the opposite slope toward the girl while the other two rode to the end of the slope to cut her off.

The Cheyenne girl, almost at the bottom of the slope, continued running toward the small ravine. She started to turn to the right, saw the one trooper coming fast at her, and spun the other way. Her ankle turned under her and she gave a short cry of pain as she fell and rolled to the bottom of the slope. She rose, starting to run, but with a limp now, and the first trooper, who had sergeant's insignia on the sleeve of his blue uniform, was upon her. He reached down to catch her but she managed to spin away from him. She began limping in the other direction only to see the other two troopers blocking her way. She tried to climb up the slope but this time the sergeant brought his horse around to strike her a glancing blow.

She sprawled forward and the other two troopers came up. Fargo watched all three leap from their horses. The sergeant, a beefy-faced man with a stocky build, reached her first and flung her to the ground. She landed on her back and he leaped onto her at once. Fargo saw the girl bring her leg up to knee her attacker but the man twisted and she struck only the side of his thigh. "Try again, squaw bitch," the trooper laughed, and he pressed her back again on the ground. Still she struggled in fury. "Get over here and hold her damn arms," the sergeant yelled. The other two hurried over to take the girl's arms and pull them up over her head. The beefy-faced sergeant pushed the deerskin garment up, and Fargo caught the flash of lithe, coppery-skinned legs.

What was taking place before him was contrary to all army regulations, to say nothing of human decency. But he wasn't about to go shooting at U.S. Cavalry troopers without knowing a lot more than he did. That could get a man into a lot of trouble. The beefy-faced one atop the girl and the other two all looked up as Fargo came down the slope. "That'll be enough, Sergeant," Fargo said quietly as he reined to a halt.

The man didn't move. Neither did the two troopers holding the girl's arms, and Fargo glanced at her and saw the uncertain pleading in the jet-black eyes. "Keep riding and fast, mister," the sergeant snarled from atop the young woman. "This is army business."

"No shit. Looks sort of personal to me," the big man atop the pinto commented.

"We're interrogating her," the sergeant snapped.

"What page would that be in the army manual?" Fargo asked blandly.

"My page, smart-ass," the man said, his beefy face growing redder. "You riding or do we take care of you, too?"

"I'll be more trouble. Guaranteed," Fargo said.

"Get his ass," the sergeant barked to his two men. "I'll keep hold of her."

The other two let go of the girl's arms and bounded to their feet. One was thin and tall, the other medium height, and Fargo watched the two men come toward him and separate to rush him from both sides. They didn't pick up their rifles, he noted. They didn't want shooting for their reasons and he didn't want any for his, not till he knew more. He waited atop the Ovaro and, at a grunt from the tall one, both rushed at him from different sides. Fargo dug his heels into the Ovaro's side. The horse reared and the two troopers automatically ducked away. The Ovaro came down hard on its powerful forelegs. At another touch from Fargo it swung its rump around, and the tall trooper flew a half-dozen feet through the air. Fargo leaped from the saddle and saw the other one coming at him from around the rear of the horse.

He held a knife in his right hand—a standard, army-issue all-purpose bivouac knife, Fargo saw. Knees bent and arms hanging loosely, Fargo let the man lunge. He measured split seconds and twisted his upper body six inches to the right as the man struck. He felt the knife blade whistle past his ear, and then he was bringing his hand up, closing an iron grip around the man's arm. He twisted, brought his other arm across, and the trooper went spinning. Fargo dropped low and threw a right into the man's midsection. The soldier dropped to one knee with a grunt. Fargo's kick sent the knife flying from his hand. The man dived for the knife as it skittered away but Fargo quickly and lightly grabbed him by the shoulder and spun him around.

A short left hook split the skin on his cheekbone. He staggered and a short, driving right cross smashed into his face. His nose erupted claret as his eyes crossed and he went down. Fargo turned in time to see the tall trooper rushing at him and he backed away. With a quick glance, he saw the sergeant still holding the girl down, still straddling her, but the soldier was watching the fight taking place alongside him. Fargo ducked under two long-armed punches the tall trooper threw, trying to use his reach advantage. Fargo feinted and the man let go with two more long blows, which were thrown from too far back with little power left in them. Fargo blocked them easily. He backed again, then again, and the trooper came after him, growing stupidly bold. He swung again and Fargo ducked, but this time his left shot out and smashed into the side of the man's jaw. The trooper grunted, staggered sideways, and Fargo's looping right instantly slammed into the man's eye.

The tall, thin form went down with blood streaming from a gash over his eye and Fargo saw the beefy-faced sergeant push up from the girl and rush forward.

"Goddamn," the man snarled and drew the gun

from its holster; it was a standard-issue army holster pistol, a six-shot, single-action weapon. But the man held it by the rounded barrel to use the long, heavy butt as a club. Clearly he still wanted no shots. He roared, catapulted his thickset body forward and brought the gun butt down in an arc. Fargo drew back his head to avoid the blow, then twisted aside as the man's charge carried him forward. He stuck a foot out to trip the man and the soldier stumbled but avoided falling. Fargo tried to wrap an arm around the sergeant's neck but had to fling himself backward as the man sent the gun butt in a flat arc. The sergeant was quicker than he looked, and Fargo had to duck away again from another fast, short blow that grazed his shoulder.

"Fucking busybody," he heard the man mutter as another chopping blow of the gun butt came at him. This time he swung a short left to the man's ribs. The trooper winced as he swung the gun butt again, upward this time, and Fargo barely avoided the blow as it grazed his jaw. The blow had left the man off balance and Fargo swung his right arm in a tremendous roundhouse punch that caught the soldier on the point of his chin. The trooper staggered, somehow avoided going down, and tried to bring the gun butt up again, but now his arm moved slowly. Fargo's blow crossed over the man's arm and landed flush in the center of his face. The beefy face grew red as a dozen little blood vessels broke and the thickset figure collapsed. He half sat, half lay on the grass, shaking his head.

His gun was on the ground now. Fargo kicked it aside as he strode past, his eyes sweeping the small ravine for the Indian girl. She had run off—limped off, he corrected himself as he swung onto the Ovaro and instantly picked up the marks of her trail. She'd gone into tall brush and he followed, noticing where she'd bent back young growths as she hurried onward. The brush ended at another downward slope of land that broke off into gulleys on all sides, but her prints were fresh and clear. He caught up to her as she neared a small brook. When she heard him approach she turned shrinking back against a mound of earth, and he saw her pick up a rock in one hand.

He slowed to a halt and swung from the saddle to see fear, defiance, and uncertainty all shouldering each other in her face. It was a handsome face, even-featured with an unusually delicate nose and wide-spaced eyes, well-fleshed lips, and good high cheekbones to carry it all off. Definitely Cheyenne, he told himself, in her height and her features. The majority of the tribes were only forty-five to seventy percent full-bloodied, someone had found in a survey, but the Cheyenne, Wichita, and Arapaho were some ninety percent full-blooded.

"I won't hurt you," he said, using sign language to emphasize his words. The Cheyenne used the Algonquian tongue and he spoke enough of it to get along, though not so well as he did the Siouan language. She blinked but he saw her relax. She straightened up and stepped toward him. He motioned to the rock in her hand and she dropped it. High, round breasts were thrusting forward even under the deerskin dress.

"You save me from your own bluecoats," she said, and the question hung in her statement.

"They were doing wrong," he said.

"Your people," she said with cold disdain, the black eyes finding icy fire.

"Are there not Cheyenne who do wrong?" he asked, and she took in his answer without showing anything in her handsome face. "Why did they chase you?" he questioned.

"They saw me," she said, telling him that was reason enough. "There were three of us. We ran in different ways."

"All beautiful squaws?" he pressed.

"Two old woman. We were digging camass root. We went too far." She took a step and he saw her wince at the pain in her ankle. It had begun to swell and lose its slenderness, he saw. He stepped back and swung onto the Ovaro and held out one hand.

"Come. You can ride with me," he said. She searched his face for a long moment and then stepped to the horse, ignoring the pain of her ankle. She had a decidedly regal bearing. Any fear she had was wrapped in quiet strength. But this was not unusual for a Cheyenne, he knew. He helped her swing onto the horse. She chose to sit behind him in the saddle, and he smelled fresh lemon oil on her. The scent was quietly provocative. She pointed south and he followed a gulley to where it widened into a gently hilly plain. She rode in silence, not touching his back, and when he reached a stand of cottonwoods her hand pressed his elbow and he halted. She let him help her swing down from the horse and he dismounted with her.

"They would have killed me, your bluecoats," she said softly, and he saw no gain in denying what was probably the truth.

"They are not my bluecoats," he said.

Her eyes, round and black and grave, stayed on him. She put her hands together in a sign of gratitude. "You are good," she said simply.

"And you are very beautiful." He smiled. "What do your people call you?"

"Red Flower," she said and waited.

"Fargo . . . Skye Fargo," he said. "Some call me the one who makes trails . . . the Trailsman." She took in his answer and nodded slowly. "I can take you further," he offered.

"No," she said, and he smiled. Trust went only so far. He understood.

"Red Flower will remember," she said and he understood her meaning. She was in his debt. He watched her walk into the cottonwoods, tall and straight, allowing only a slight concession to the sore ankle. When she vanished in the trees he climbed back into the saddle and rode back at a fast canter. He wasn't surprised when he reached the small ravine below the ridge. The three troopers were gone, and he spat to one side as he sent the Ovaro up to the top of the ridge line. The army was made up mostly of good, dedicated men, decent and honorable men. But it had its share of misfits, especially out here where they sent the bottom of the barrel.

Still, these three hadn't been riding in this country alone. He halted at the end of the ridge and scanned the land that spread out below—rolling hills, good tree cover but plenty of open land. This was fertile land, rich enough to offer food, clothing, and shelter to last through the harsh winters. Land of the mountains, Montana, the early Spanish explorers had named it and aptly enough, for to the west the towering Rockies reached up to touch the sky. He had seen small game all over as he'd ridden, plus plenty of bear and elk, weasel and marten, and in the crystal clear lakes, pike and muskellunge bigger than a fat beaver. He had come off a trail drive up from south Wyoming and was close enough to visit Betty Harrison. She had come out here with a husband who got himself killed trying to saddlebreak a sunfisher. But she'd stayed on, hired some hands, and made a go of a small ranch. Fargo smiled as he thought about Betty Harrison.

He'd known her back in Kansas before she thought of marrying.

Full-bosomed, always a tad on the heavy side, Betty was every bit as willing and eager as she'd ever been when he appeared at the ranch. Maybe more so, he murmured silently, and they had turned the clock back together, a clock made of pillowy breasts and large, soft lips, of hips wide and full and made for riding. There'd never been any false modesty about Betty Harrison. There still wasn't, and the visit had been all any man could want. When he'd left, he'd decided to circle north. It had been a good while since he'd ridden the north Montana Territory, like Betty Harrison it hadn't changed much.

It was still a land that, with the snap of a finger, could take your breath away with its beauty and your life away with its danger. That had been reaffirmed in the flame-tipped beauty of the wild columbine and the burned-out Conestogas he had passed, in the red-purple brilliance of the blazing star, and the arrows imbedded in charred cabins. It was still a land where calm was but a thin veil over fury. His reflections snapped off as he spotted the sign he had been seeking—a thin column of dust in the distance. He watched the column head east, spurred the Ovaro from the ridge, and let the horse out into a full gallop when he reached the rolling terrain below. The line of dust grew more distinct as he closed distance, and he slowed to a halt when the dust turned into a column of U.S. Cavalry in their blue-and-gold uniforms.

He counted sixteen troopers, with one officer riding lead at the head of the column, and he waited as they rode up to a halt. "Afternoon," Fargo said pleasantly as his eyes swept over the column. He didn't have to look beyond the three troopers directly behind the officer. The tall, thin one wore a bandage over his right eye, the one beside him a patch on his split cheek and another on his nose. The sergeant's face was swollen and bruised, his lips thickened and puffy.

"Captain Burton Cogswell," the officer said, and Fargo saw imperiousness in a face too young to have earned it. The man's very crisp manner marked him as the product of an eastern officer's school, most likely West Point. "You been riding alone through here?" the captain asked, and Fargo nodded. "See any Cheyenne?" Cogswell asked.

"Nope," Fargo said blandly.

"Three of my men I sent ahead as scouts were attacked," the captain said. "They were ambushed by six of the damn savages."

Fargo let his eyes move slowly across the three troopers. "Six?" he remarked and saw each of the three men avoid his eyes. "How come they were beat on instead of just killed?" he asked the captain.

"The Cheyenne obviously wanted to take prisoners," Cogswell said with a trace of impatience. "Apparently you don't know the Indian, mister."

"I know the Indian a damn sight better than you do, I'd wager," Fargo said and let a smile take the edge off his words. Captain Burton Cogswell fastened him with a stony stare.

"What's your name, mister? And how do you know the Indian so well?" he pushed forward.

"Fargo . . . Skye Fargo. Some call me the Trailsman. You can ask General Leeds about me. He still commander in the territory?" Fargo asked.

"Yes, but he works out of Fort Ellis," Cogswell said and Fargo smiled inwardly. The mention of General Leeds had made the captain draw back some. "How do you come to know the general?" Cogswell queried.

"Did some special assignments for him," Fargo answered.

"We're operating out of a small field post near Desmond Kray's trading post. There's half a town there. You know Kray?" the Captain asked.

"Never met him."

"We're riding back to post. You're welcome to ride along with us if you've a mind for your scalp," Cogswell said.

"You having troubles?" Fargo questioned as he swung the Ovaro alongside the captain's mount.

"I'm trying to keep some discipline around here," Cogswell said. The imperiousness was quick to return to his voice, Fargo noted. "Authority and force, that's what these damn Cheyennes understand," Cogswell said.

"I know the Northern Cheyenne. Disciplining them could be walking a tightrope," Fargo suggested.

"No tightrope for me." The captain bristled. "There are a number of settlers now in this region and they look to the army for protection. I intend to see that they get it."

He waved the column forward, and Fargo's glance went to the sergeant and the two other battered troopers. Their cut and swollen faces didn't hide the nervous apprehension in their eyes. Fargo decided to remain silent—for now, anyway. If the captain was facing real trouble with the Cheyenne he'd need every body and gun in his command.

2

Captain Cogswell's riding form echoed his bearing, Fargo took note. He sat on his bay army mount with commanding arrogance, stiff-backed and rigid, his jaw thrust forward and his gray eyes steely as they swept over the terrain. The captain was a man not just in love with his own authority but filled with a private anger, Fargo decided.

"What's the size of your command here, Captain?" Fargo queried.

"Fifty line troopers, four older men assigned to stable duty, one smithy, one cook and a helper and a company doc," the captain said.

"Fifty-eight total," Fargo said and tucked the figure away in a corner of his mind. He had the strange feeling it would be important to remember.

"You staying around here, Fargo?" the captain asked.

"Haven't decided."

"Then you don't have another trail job lined up," Cogswell noted.

"Not for now," Fargo said.

"Then you'll be moving on tomorrow," the captain said.

The man was full of questions, perhaps too many. An inner voice told Fargo to be cautious. " 'Less I fall into a job suddenly and that's not likely," he said.

"There's a half a town alongside the command post.

They call it Kray's Corners. Man named Desmond Kray runs the trading post and inn. Small place, not more than six rooms, but they're seldom all filled. I'm sure you'll be able to get one if you want to spend the night," the captain said, seeming to relax some.

"If I decide," Fargo said and saw the low silhouette of the buildings come into sight. They grew larger as he neared and he saw the army barracks alongside the handful of buildings, a line of wood barracks with the stables opposite them. There was a company pennant flying over the captain's quarters. The captain came up beside him as he drew to a halt, and the squad of troopers rode into the barracks area. Fargo saw the three men fasten him with their gaze again, their eyes still full of apprehension. They were plainly uneasy, afraid of what he might say and unable to understand why he'd stayed silent this long. He kept his face a mask as he dismounted and turned away.

The doors of the trading post were open, flanked with axes, shovels, boots, blankets, and rifles, and a half-dozen Indian bearskin robes. The inn, a ramshackle structure, rose up alongside the store. "Who does he get for customers around here?" Fargo asked Cogswell.

"Mostly drummers and trappers, but there are enough new settlers in need of a place to stay while they find their own piece of land. And there's a stage once a month that comes by," the captain added as a tall, thin figure hurried from the store. The man's black hair was worn long, and he had beetling black brows on a sharp-nosed face with small, darting eyes. Fargo saw the man instantly take in the Ovaro with a covetous glance. "This is Desmond Kray," said the captain. "Skye Fargo, here. Man said he might want a room for the night."

Desmond Kray nodded. "We've room," he said.

"Good," said Fargo, nodding, and Kray led the way to the inn, where Fargo followed him into a common eating room with two long wooden tables and backless chairs. A row of room keys hung on a pegboard against one wall, and Desmond Kray handed him a heavy key.

"Last room down the hall. You'll be facing a lean-to in the back where you can stable your horse," the man said.

"Sounds fine," Fargo said as a woman with black hair and a flat-featured, olive-skinned face appeared. She carried thirty pounds too much on her short figure and wore a gray blouse over her heavy, hanging breasts.

"My woman, Rosita," Desmond Kray said. "Bought her in Mexico five years ago. She'll get you food and drink when you want." He turned to the captain. "Now for important business. You get any of them today?" he questioned.

"No, the patrol was uneventful," the captain said.

"I tell you, patrolling's not worth a damn. You have to go after them, slaughter them, hit their camps," Kray said.

"Desmond's talking about the Northern Cheyenne," the captain said to Fargo. "They stole his niece, Arlene. She worked here."

"She went out for a walk one afternoon. That's the last we saw of her. They took her, the murdering savages. She was only one more. They raid the settlers regularly. I'm demanding the captain wipe them out. That's the only answer," Kray said.

"I'm afraid I agree with Desmond," Cogswell put in. "This has gone on long enough. I'm going to put an end to it. I'm going to teach them who's in charge here."

Fargo let his lips purse. "That approach could get an awful lot of people killed," he said.

"They're being killed now," Desmond Kray noted.

"I know that, but that's not a wholesale massacre, which you could trigger," Fargo said.

"Sounds like you're afraid, mister," Kray said, a sneer in his voice.

"I like keeping my scalp," Fargo said.

"Then just light on out of here. This is none of your concern, anyway," Kray bristled.

Fargo smiled. "Once in a while I get civic-minded."

"What's that mean?" Kray frowned, his beetling black eyebrows coming together.

"It means once in a while I get to feel I ought to do a good deed, sort of make up for all the other kind I've done," Fargo said.

"The northern Cheyenne don't need any good deeds," Kray snarled. "You some damn Indian lover, Fargo?"

"Wasn't thinking about the Cheyenne. This morning, before I ran into the captain and his troop, I came onto three families visiting together. There were seven of the nicest little kids you ever saw, playing in an old Bucks County hay wagon. I'd hate to see them all massacred in a Cheyenne uprising."

"I don't expect to let that happen, Fargo," the captain said with an edge of chiding patience in his voice.

"Sometimes, you light a match it can set off a forest fire," Fargo said.

"Well, I'm not forgetting what they did to Arlene, not on your damn life. I want every last one of them killed, especially that damn Red Bull," Kray thundered.

"Desmond's referring to a warrior chief they call Red Bull. He's been stepping up his raiding, getting bolder and bolder. I agree with Desmond that there'll never be any peace until he's killed," the captain said.

"Sometimes even the bloodthirstiest can be reached. I managed that one time for General Leeds. It'd be worth a try," Fargo said.

"He's killed everybody who's ever tried to deal with him," Kray snapped. "There'll be no reaching him and no point in trying."

"Again, I'm afraid I go along with that. I'm especially bothered by the fact that he's suddenly grown more aggressive," the captain said. "I'm going to initiate an all-out campaign against him, wipe out all of his people. I'll bring some law and order to this territory."

Fargo shrugged. Desmond Kray was hell-bent on personal revenge and the captain was convinced he could wipe out this warrior chief. Their attitudes seemed to be reinforcing each other. Fargo decided he'd stay a spell. He needed no better reason than the kids in the hay wagon, but, in addition, his curiosity had been aroused.

He knew that time and events had a way of bringing sense to the most stubborn of men. He offered the captain a slow smile. "Your show," he said. "But I'll help if you want."

"Your help won't be necessary, Fargo," Captain Cogswell said brusquely and walked from the inn.

"This ain't any of your business. Stay the hell out of it, mister," Desmond Kray said in his ear.

Fargo kept his smile. "Maybe," he said. "But I don't often do what I'm told to do."

He started to turn away when he saw the figure standing half in the shadows: a young woman, tall, standing so silent and motionless that he hadn't noticed her till now. He took in shoulder-length light brown hair, big, round, brown eyes, and full lips, a round-cheeked face that was softly pretty yet not without a quiet strength. A shapeless brown dress could not hide the long curve of her thighs or the high thrust of her breasts. Fargo's eyes flicked questioningly to Kray.

"Her name's Amanda. She's my scullery girl. You can talk to her but don't expect an answer," Kray said. "She can hear but she doesn't talk or write."

"Can't talk or doesn't?" Fargo asked.

"Damned if I know. She was the only one alive in a wagon train attacked by the Cheyenne. Arlene took her in three years ago," Kray said. "She's never made a sound. But she can make herself understood. She has her own ways."

"She hasn't talked since the wagon train attack?" asked Fargo.

"That's right. But for all we know she was always that way," Kray said. Fargo glanced at the young woman and found the soft, round eyes appraising him as surely as he was appraising her.

"Hello, Amanda," he said, and she nodded back and dropped her glance.

"The damn floor's dirty. Clean it," Kray barked at her, and Fargo saw her turn away and walk to a corner where a bucket and a mop rested. Her quick glance at Kray contained both fear and dislike.

"How'd you learn her name?" Fargo asked as he walked outside with Kray.

"She wore a bracelet with her name on it," Kray said and strode away to the trading post. Fargo took hold of the Ovaro's reins to lead the horse to the rear of the house and he saw the young girl starting to mop the floor. He'd known of victims struck dumb by a terrible attack. Most of them had been children but he had seen a few young women unable to talk. Something snapped inside them, a doc had explained to him once. Sometimes they felt guilty for having survived. He glanced into the inn again and saw Amanda's eyes on him as she mopped the floor, and again he saw something more than curiosity in the deep, dark orbs.

He led the Ovaro away to the rear of the house. There he found the lean-to, lifted the saddle off, and gave the horse a quick rubdown with the body brush he took from his saddlebag. When he was finished, the dusk had turned into night and the barracks area still showed lamplight in every barrack. When he crossed back three troopers were huddled outside one of the barracks. The door was open and emitted enough light for him to recognize the beefy-faced sergeant and the other two. They saw him, looked away, and hurried inside. Fargo gave a grim grunt as he walked on. They were still trying to figure out why he hadn't turned them in, and they were still nervous about it. They deserved to stew in their own pot, he thought, and he stepped into the inn.

The heavyset Mexican woman was there, and he asked for food. She gestured for him to sit at one of the long tables and hurried into the kitchen. He smelled the stew in a few moments, and it wasn't a long wait before she returned with a bowl and a kettle. She set the bowl in front of him and filled it from the kettle, and he was hungry enough not to worry about the contents; it tasted edible. He was halfway through when the girl appeared with a pitcher of water and poured a glass for him. He watched her move with quiet gracefulness and decided she was more attractive than average. He guessed her age at about nineteen, which would have made her sixteen at the time of the attack, certainly young enough for her to have been struck mute.

"Is Amanda really your name?" he asked, and she nodded.

"Did you ever know how to talk, Amanda?" he asked, and he saw her face set as she turned away from him with no gesture of any kind. Was the question one she refused to answer, he wondered, or did she simply resent it? She hurried from the room, plainly unwilling to stay for any more questions.

Fargo finished the meal and felt the tiredness of the long day's ride pulling at him. He went to the room at the end of the corridor. It was a small space, with barely room for a cot, a battered dresser, and washbasin. The lone window, he saw, did look out over the lean-to, and he saw the Ovaro standing quietly a dozen yards away.

Fargo undressed, hung his gunbelt on the edge of the cot at the front corner, and stretched out in the darkness. The night stayed warm and he fell asleep quickly, glad to close out the world. He had slept well into the night when he came awake, a familiar sound penetrating his subconscious. He sat up in the cot, ears straining, and it came again—the Ovaro blowing air, shuffling its feet nervously. Fargo swung long legs from the bed as he heard the horse snort again. There was alarm in the sound, and he yanked on trousers as he went to the window. He found the Ovaro at once. The horse was moving nervously on the long tether. Something had spooked him, Fargo knew, and he peered across the dark land, which was dimly lighted by a half-moon.

Rather than take the long way down the corridor and out the front door, Fargo opened the window further and swung himself from the room. He touched the ground on the balls of his feet, dropped into a half-crouch, and frowned across the ground toward the trees. His eyes swept back and forth, searching for movement, perhaps the silent forms of a wolf pack or the lumbering bulk of a grizzly. Mountain lions seldom came this close to people, but there was always the exception. But he saw nothing that moved. He rose, stepped to the horse, and ran one hand along the animal's powerful, jet-black neck. The horse grew calmer at once, but his ears still twitched, and Fargo kept his hand on the strong neck as he let his gaze sweep the treeline again.

Still, nothing moved. "It's gone, whatever it was, old friend," Fargo murmured. "Easy does it." He stroked the horse's neck a moment longer and turned away to climb back through the window. He had taken but three steps when the voice broke the stillness.

"Don't move, mister," it said. "Put your hands on your head." Fargo halted, froze in place. "Now, dammit," the voice rasped. Fargo lifted his hands as he obeyed and glimpsed the figure out of his peripheral vision. The man stood at the corner of the building. He had been hiding around the other side, it was obvious. He stepped up directly behind Fargo, who felt the man reach out and pull the Colt out of its holster. "Move over to your horse," the man said, and again Fargo obeyed. When he reached the Ovaro he turned to see a medium-sized man wearing a narrow-brimmed Stetson and everyday cowpoke's clothes. The man held a Joslyn army revolver, five-shot single action, a powerful enough gun but slow-firing, no gunslinger's weapon. It marked him at once as cheap hired help. But he held the gun steady as he rasped out orders and Fargo saw the dun-colored horse move out from behind the building.

The man swung onto the horse without taking his gun from its target, Fargo noted. "You been moving back and forth behind the house," Fargo said.

"That's right, enough to get your horse nervous," the man said.

"And you expected that'd bring me out," Fargo nodded.

"It did, didn't it?" the man snorted smugly.

"It did," Fargo conceded. "Why? Or maybe you've made a mistake."

"No mistake. Get on your horse. You can ride him bareback," the man said. Fargo untethered the pinto and swung onto the horse. The man steered his horse in a half-circle and came near enough for Fargo to see a tight, thin face under the brim of the hat. The man brought his horse around behind him, Fargo saw. "Ride in front of me, nice and slow. Head for that tree line," the voice ordered.

Fargo spoke over his shoulder as he moved the Ovaro forward and the man fell in behind him. "You going to shoot me go and do it," he said. "I've no favorite place for getting shot."

"Not here," the man said.

"Why not?" Fargo tossed back.

"Orders," the answer came and Fargo let his thoughts leapfrog. Whoever had done the hiring didn't want a body on hand to trigger questions. Fargo let a hard smile edge his lips as he walked the horse forward. The man had orders not to put a bullet into his back until they were plenty deep in the woods. Maybe that grim fact also held a way out. He'd have to gamble that the man would hold off shooting. It was a hell of a gamble, but it was his only chance.

He slowly straightened his legs, held them out sideways, and then brought them hard into the Ovaro's lower ribs. The horse shot forward and Fargo brought the reins around to slap them hard against its neck. "Goddamn," he heard the man hiss, but the Ovaro was into a full gallop as he flattened himself against the powerful jet neck. "Son of a bitch," he heard the voice rasp and then the sound of the other horse giving chase. But the woods were close and Fargo kept the pinto at a full run as he charged into the tree line, skirted a grainy elm, and dodged around another. He slowed but only enough to avoid smashing into the thick tree trunks as the forest grew more dense and the moonlight grew paler. He had guessed right and he was still alive because of it.

But he was still unarmed and being chased by a man carrying two guns, and he heard his pursuer crashing through the forest after him. The man was angry but confident, Fargo knew, certain that it was but a matter of time before he'd catch up to his unarmed quarry. Ordinarily he'd have a right to his confidence. But he didn't really know who he was chasing. Fargo maneuvered the pinto between two large box elder as his gaze lifted upward to sweep the low branches of the trees. He spotted one that fitted his needs and, without slowing the horse's pace even a step, he rose in the stirrups, twisted his long, well-muscled frame, and leaped from the saddle.

He landed on the balls of his feet as the Ovaro kept going. Then he whirled, closed both hands around the low branch of the tree, and swung himself upward. He had his legs wrapped around the branch and was pulling himself up onto the next one when his pursuer thundered by below, following the sound of the Ovaro. Fargo climbed onto a third branch that was wide and heavy with leaves and flattened himself out amongst the thick foliage. The Ovaro would come to a halt in moments, he knew, and the man would reach the riderless horse. Then the chase would end and the hunt begin. The man was already making another mistake. He thought he was the hunter.

Fargo lay still, listening, and heard the hoofbeats come to a halt. The man had come upon the Ovaro. Fargo shifted to a more comfortable position on the branch and settled down to wait. It wasn't a long wait. He heard the man's voice in the distance, then the slow steps of the horse as its rider moved back the way he had come. The man paused after every few steps to listen. Finally he came into sight, still stopping the horse after every few steps to strain his ears. He held the Joslyn in his hand, prepared to fire at the first sound out of the brush.

He moved his horse in small circles, Fargo noticed as the man strained his ears and halted a dozen feet away. "Come on out and maybe we can make a deal," the man called, cocking his head to listen and straightening it when there was no answer. "Come on, don't be stupid. This is the best chance you're gonna get," the man tried again. Once more he waited, listened, and moved the horse another few steps. His slow circle would finally bring him very close to the tree where he lay hidden, Fargo saw. He remained motionless, waiting, and the man continued his careful circle. The man raised his voice again. "I figure there's another hour or so till daylight. Your little game's over then. Come out now and we can deal," he offered.

Fargo snorted silently. The man was right about what daylight would bring. He'd have to make his move before that happened. Fargo's eyes followed the rider below as the man drew closer. He half rose on his perch as the man halted again, perhaps two feet to the left of the tree. Moving with careful deliberateness so as not to rustle a leaf, Fargo swung to the branch directly below. He pressed his feet firmly against the branch, measuring the dip in it before releasing his hold on the branch above. His movements were studied but they took only seconds. The man had started to move forward again and he'd be out of range in moments. Fargo saw his Colt tucked into the man's belt as the horse passed a few feet in front of where he hung in the tree. The rider would be out of range in another thirty seconds. Fargo swore silently. He tensed his muscles, used his arms to swing himself, and then he was hurtling forward feet first through the air.

The man caught the rush of air and half turned in the saddle as Fargo slammed into him feet first. Fargo twisted his body to brace for the fall and glimpsed the man flying forward off the horse. His own shoulders hit the horse's rump as he went backward, and he brought his arms in against his body as he hit the ground. He landed hard but compactly, rolled, and came up on one knee to see the man starting to turn himself around. The Joslyn had skittered from the man's hand and lay on the ground not more than a dozen feet from him. Fargo flung himself forward in a headlong dive, arms outstretched, and his hand had just closed around the revolver when he saw the man yank the Colt from his belt. No time to aim, Fargo rolled, the Joslyn in his grip. He hit the brush at the base of a line of box elder as he heard the Colt erupt.

Two shots tore through the brush, neither too close, and the man fired again, two more shots sent in a spray pattern. These came closer and Fargo flattened himself into the brush, spun himself around on his stomach, and brought the Joslyn up to fire. He wanted the man alive to answer questions, but the figure was rushing toward him, the Colt held out to fire again. Fargo squinted in the dimness, aimed for the man's leg, and fired. He was unused to the pistol; the shot went wide, and he fired again. The second bullet grazed the man's leg, but he was racing at him and firing the Colt as he ran. Fargo swore as a bullet slammed into the tree an inch from his head and he flung himself backward as the second shot whistled into the ground where he had just been.

But the man had fired off six shots. He had nothing left in the Colt and Fargo rose as the figure charged through the brush at him. "The next one's in your gut," he said as the man came to a halt, the Colt still in his hand. "You give me some answers and you can ride away alive," Fargo said.

The man shrugged. "Why not?" he muttered. Fargo took a step closer. Then he caught the twitch of the man's arm as he brought it up in a short, sudden motion. Fargo had only a moment to see the empty revolver hurtling through the air at him and had to twist his head away or take the gun full in the face. The revolver flew past his ear as he heard the man charging, and he turned just as the figure barreled into him. Fargo went backward from the force of the man's bull-like charge but he had brought the revolver up, his finger on the trigger. His reaction was purely instinctive and automatic as his finger tightened on the trigger. The shot was muffled against the man's belly but Fargo heard the gasp of pain and felt the figure go limp instantly.

"Ah, damn," Fargo spit out as the man sank to the ground, both hands clutching his abdomen. He rolled onto his back and drew his knees up, but his legs fell forward at once. Fargo dropped to one knee beside him and saw the glassiness already forming over the man's eyes. "Damn fool," he muttered. "Damn fool." The man was still breathing—short, wheezing gasps—and Fargo leaned closer to him. "Who hired you, dammit?" he asked. "Who paid you?" The man's eyes stared back at him. Suddenly they were blank, and the short, wheezing gasps ended. Fargo swore inwardly. He'd no feelings of sympathy for the man who, he knew, would have shot him in the back without a second thought for his thirty pieces of silver. Yet it had all ended pointlessly with nothing out of it for anyone.

He pulled his lips back in distaste as he went through the dead man's pockets and found nothing to identify him. Then he pushed to his feet, retrieved his Colt, and reloaded while he whistled softly. The Ovaro appeared in moments and Fargo pulled himself onto the horse. He tried to sort out his thoughts as he rode back and realized he had very little to sort out. There were only two facts. Someone had been hired to kill him and the attempt had failed. But who had done the hiring? There was little question that the three troopers were the prime candidates. Even though he hadn't turned them in yet, they were plainly afraid he might still do it. Or maybe they feared he'd try to hold it over their heads in some way. Having him killed would end all their problems.

His lips pursed in thought. It was also the kind of desperate stunt three such mean-minded, fearful men would do. They had to stay the likeliest suspects, but he found himself thinking about Desmond Kray. The man had become astonishingly angry at any attempt to dissuade the captain from a campaign against the Cheyenne. Maybe he had so much hate inside him he'd kill rather than let anyone interfere with it. He had seen men like that, Fargo reflected, and he decided he couldn't entirely rule out Desmond Kray. That left Captain Burton Cogswell. He also plainly resented any interference with his plans to mount an attack against the Cheyenne. But a stiff-backed ego didn't equate with murder. He'd discount the captain, Fargo decided.

He turned off further speculation as the dark bulk of the inn came into sight. He tethered the Ovaro under the lean-to again and climbed back into his room through the window. Shedding his trousers, he sank down on the cot with only one thing clear in his mind. His decision to stay awhile longer had been very personally reinforced. He had a score to settle.

3

Morning came in warm and sunny and Fargo found Kray's woman had a big enameled coffeepot on the table in the front room. He poured a mug for himself and had almost finished sipping the strong, bracing brew when the young woman appeared, a splint broom in one hand. She had changed from the shapeless brown garment to a gray one almost equally shapeless, but once again Fargo saw the silent gracefulness in her movements. " 'Morning, Amanda," he said. Her lovely face showed no expression but she returned an almost imperceptible nod.

Fargo's glance went to the doorway as Desmond Kray entered. The sharp-faced man fastened a belligerent stare on him, and Fargo couldn't determine if there was surprise in the darting eyes.

"You moving on?" Kray barked.

"Decided to stay awhile," Fargo said. " 'Less you don't want any boarders."

"Your money's as good as anybody's so long as you mind your own damn business," Desmond Kray growled.

"Whatever that turns out to be," Fargo said blandly and drew a narrow-eyed glance from Kray as the man stalked away. Fargo finished the last of the coffee and saw Amanda watching him, a silent, appraising thoughtfulness in her eyes.

"Get some water in the trough," Kray's voice called

from outside and she turned away. Fargo strolled from the inn. The young woman's thoughtful eyes stayed with him. He went to the Ovaro, saddled the horse, and fed him some oats at an oat bin alongside the barracks as he watched the squad preparing their mounts to go on patrol. The three troopers were there but he saw only furtiveness in their glances. It was probably too late to find surprise, he told himself. The hired gun would have reported back by now if he'd succeeded. Fargo started to lead the pinto away when he saw the uniformed figure coming toward him. He wore a captain's bars, but was a shorter man, graying, with a tired face.

"Captain Schroder, company physician," the man introduced himself.

"My pleasure," Fargo said.

"You must be the man that rode in with the patrol yesterday," the doctor said, his eyes studying the big man.

"I am," Fargo said.

"Captain Cogswell seems to think you're an Indian lover or a coward," the doctor said, his eyes continuing to appraise him. "I've learned something about reading a man. Somehow, you don't seem to fit either of those roles."

"You're right there, Doc," Fargo agreed.

"Something you said gave the captain those ideas," Schroder smiled.

"The captain made his own conclusions," Fargo shrugged. "I told him his plans could trigger a full-scale Cheyenne uprising."

"Good God, I hope not." The doctor frowned. "I've no staff. I'm waiting for the army to send me an assistant but they haven't done so yet. You know how slow the army can be." Fargo nodded and the army doctor let himself look uncertain. "Of course, I'm not informed enough to know whether you're right or wrong."

"I'm informed enough," Fargo said grimly and broke off the conversation. Captain Cogswell approached, riding quirt in hand, as one of the men brought his horse. "Starting your campaign, Captain?" Fargo asked.

"Not yet. I'm going to reconnoiter, first. I know they have a number of small camps scattered around. I want to get a line on them before I strike," the captain said.

"Maybe we'll meet up. I'm going to scout around some, too," Fargo said.

The captain's frown was immediate. "Why?" he questioned.

"To learn the territory. The more territories you know the better off you are in my business. You never know where you'll be called to break trail," Fargo said. The captain nodded, plainly satisfied with the answer, and swung onto his mount. Fargo watched him lead the squad away before he climbed onto the Ovaro and saw Dr. Schroder's amused smile. "You don't believe I'm going out to scout around?" Fargo questioned.

"Oh, I do. I'm just not convinced of the reason you gave the captain," Doc Schroder answered.

Fargo allowed a smile as he wheeled the pinto around. "We'll talk again," he said.

"Any time." The doctor smiled and Fargo rode from the barracks area. He saw the column of dust raised by the captain and his squad, rode parallel to it for a spell, and then turned into the heavier tree cover. He slowed to a walk, picked his way through the forestland, his eyes seeking the little things that the captain and his patrol would never pick up. He found them as he wandered—the print of mocassins, some smaller than others, women's footprints, a piece of hair braid, a snippet of torn leather from a calfskin pouch. He didn't press on to find the camp he knew was not too far away. He didn't want any incidents. He turned and rode out of the heavy tree cover onto higher, hillier land.

He could still see the dust column of the captain's squad. They had turned and were heading in his direction. Fargo's gaze went to the dry ground where he saw the prints of unshod Indian ponies. The captain had also picked up enough to turn him this way, and Fargo rode higher, behind a rock formation where the pony prints moved downward into a shallow valley dotted with stands of black oak and cottonwood. Another Cheyenne encampment lay in the valley somewhere, Fargo realized. The captain would conclude as much, also, when he reached here and Fargo turned the pinto and sent the horse west in a trot.

None of the indications he'd seen anywhere marked a main line camp. He hadn't seen enough pony prints for that. These were small work camps for skinning and drying hides and furs and meat. They were set up so the hunters wouldn't have to drag whole carcasses all the way back to the main camp.

Fargo kept the pinto moving westward as he followed the pony prints, and he was deep into a forest of cottonwood when his nostrils twitched. The odor of woodsmoke and hides drying on racks drifted to him on a soft breeze. He halted, marked the general location of the camp, and turned back. It was all he needed for now, the location of both camps. The day was drawing to an end when he reached Kray's Corners. The troop had already returned, the men brushing down their mounts. He unsaddled the Ovaro behind the inn, and when he strolled back he saw the captain looking pleased with himself.

"Any luck?" he inquired blandly.

"Got a line on one of their camps," Cogswell said. "I'm going to give that murdering savage a taste of his own medicine."

"You've a plan, a campaign ready?" Fargo asked.

"I certainly do. I'm going to smoke him out, make him angry enough to come after me," the captain said. "He's been raiding and killing and now taking Desmond's niece. It's about time he was stopped, once and for all."

That much was undeniably true, Fargo admitted silently. Yet it was the captain's plan for justice that still made him nervous. "If you trigger a full-scale war with the Cheyenne, how do you figure to protect the settlers and fight Red Bull with some fifty troopers?" he questioned.

The captain continued to look smug. "First of all, I estimate one U.S. Cavalry trooper is worth five undisciplined Cheyenne braves," he said.

"There are experienced Indian fighters who'd say you have that exactly backwards," Fargo commented and saw a flash of displeasure come into the captain's eyes.

"They'd be quite wrong. On top of that, I'll be using well-established military tactics," Cogswell said. "And one more ace in the hole. I'm expecting twenty-five additional troopers to arrive sometime within the next few days."

Fargo nodded appreciatively. That would make a minimum of seventy-five line troops. That would definitely give the captain a real boost in firepower. "That's reassuring," he said. "That'll give you more clout, but how will that protect the settlers scattered all around?"

"I can place three men with each settlement," the captain said.

"Three men with each family won't mean shit in a Cheyenne raid," Fargo bit out, not hiding his contempt.

"You're bent on underestimating a U.S. trooper," Cogswell snapped.

"No. You're bent on underestimating the Cheyenne," Fargo threw back. "You get twenty-five new men, you don't make them arrow fodder in twos and threes. You keep them together to help give yourself more firepower when the time comes. You'll sure as hell need it."

"You're the one who brought up protecting the homesteaders," Cogswell snapped.

"Call them in here to the barracks till this is over. That's the only way you can protect them," Fargo said.

"Thank you for all your advice, Fargo," Cogswell said, his voice dripping with sarcasm. "But I know my job here."

"Really? You could've fooled me," Fargo said.

"Meaning what?" the captain glowered.

"Meaning I thought you were supposed to put out fires, not start them," Fargo answered. The captain's jaw set tightly as he strode away.

Fargo had turned in the dusk to go into the inn when he saw the tall, slender figure in the half-shadows. She had obviously been there listening. She turned and went into the Inn a few steps in front of him. She seemed to glide, her movements graceful even inside the formless dress. She hurried across the dining room to vanish down a corridor, and Kray's woman entered with a clay urn of stew and a pitcher of water.

Fargo sat down at the table and found the stew tastier than he'd expected. "Rabbit?" he asked Rosita and the woman nodded. He was almost finished when Kray appeared and she dished a plate out for him at once. Kray ate with wolfish haste and leaned back in the chair to regard Fargo with a curious stare when he finished.

"You know, Fargo, if you had a niece carried off by those savages you wouldn't be giving the captain any lip," Kray said.

"I'm sorry for what happened to your niece. Getting a lot more people killed won't bring her back," Fargo answered.

"It'll put an end to that stinkin' savage Red Bull making off with any other young girl out for a walk alone," Kray shot back.

"Maybe other ways to get to Red Bull ought to be explored," Fargo suggested.

"There are no other ways. He's got to be wiped out, killed That's the only way," Kray insisted.

"How did Arlene come to work for you here?" Fargo asked.

"Her folks died five years ago. She had no other kin and came to visit. I needed help to look after things when I went on trips so she stayed on," Kray explained.

"She was older than Amanda, then," Fargo said.

"Maybe five years older," Kray said as he rose. "You let the captain take care of Red Bull, Fargo, or go on your way."

"That a threat?" Fargo smiled.

"It's advice," Kray said and hurried from the room.

Fargo finished the coffee before he went to his room, shed his clothes, and stretched out on the cot. He let his thoughts idle as a red wolf howled in the distance. Desmond Kray talked a lot about the loss of his niece, but revenge more than grief seemed to color his words. Cogswell appeared to be a man running on his own track, one that perhaps coincidentally paralleled Desmond Kray's. It all added up to an incendiary situation, and Fargo couldn't see a way to head it off. He'd keep trying to find a way, he promised himself, and he was about to close his eyes when he heard the knock at the door, so faint so hardly caught it.

He swung from the cot, drew on his trousers, and took the Colt from its holster hanging at the end of the cot. He opened the door and stared at the soft, round cheeks and brown eyes of Amanda. Unsmiling, she stared back, but her eyes moved down to take in the muscled symmetry of his bare torso. She lifted one arm and beckoned to him to follow. He slipped on his boots while she waited in the dark corridor, trailing her through the front room and down another corridor, where she opened a door and again beckoned him. He stepped into a large room with two large mattresses on the floor, one against the other. A lamp burning low let him see a battered dresser with a washstand atop it along with various hairbrushes and combs. Clothes hung on a cluster of wall pegs and chests, and hatboxes were neatly stacked in one corner.

"This is your room?" he asked, and she nodded. His eyes circled the room again. "You and Arlene lived here," he said and drew another nod. She turned, crossed the room, and folded her arms over her breasts as she stared at him. A tiny furrow clouded her smooth forehead. She plainly sought a way to communicate further. "What did you bring me here to tell me?" he queried gently.

She walked to the dresser and picked up a hairbrush, turned the handle to him so he could see the initial *A* on it. "You want to talk to me about Arlene," he said, and she blinked, her face remaining grave. "Go on," he urged even as he wondered how she intended to make him understand anything. She pointed to the initial again and again to run standing in place, pumping her arms and legs furiously. "Running," Fargo said, and she continued. "Arlene liked to run," he said, and she shook her head no and cast a pained glance at him. But she continued the motion of running. His eyes narrowed as he felt the thought gather inside him. "Arlene was running. Arlene ran away," he said, and she stopped and nodded vigorously.

Fargo's eyes stayed narrowed at her as she panted after the mock running and he saw her breasts rise and fall under the dress. "She didn't go for a walk," Fargo said. "She ran away." Amanda clapped her hands together in mock applause though her face stayed gravely serious. "Why did she run away?" he asked. Amanda whirled, dropped to her knees in a corner, clasped her arms around herself, and began to shake. "She was sick?" he tried. Amanda shook off the statement. His thoughts leapfrogged as she continued to hold herself and tremble. "She was afraid," he said, excited at the conclusion. Amanda stopped trembling, stood up, and applauded again.

She didn't use sign language as the Indians did, with its formalized gestures for specific words and meanings, he noted. She played her own kind of sign language, a kind of charade, and made herself understood surprisingly well. He gazed at her with admiration, put his hands on her shoulders and gently pressed her down onto a wooden stool. "Let's go over this again," Fargo said. "Arlene didn't go for a walk in the woods. She was running away and she was running because she was afraid of something."

Amanda patted his shoulder commendingly. "Why was she afraid?" he questioned and Amanda turned her palms upward in the universal sign of not knowing. "You've no idea," he said, and she shrugged helplessly. He studied her for a long moment and she stood calmly for his appraisal. "Maybe you're wrong," he said, watching for her reaction.

It came with an instant frown of protest that filled her face. She stood up and moved two fingers of one hand in a gesture of walking and pointed to him with her other hand.

"You want me to leave?" he asked.

She made another impatient face at him, paused, and then touched one hand to her forehead in the common gesture for looking and shielding one's eyes from the sun while she again let the two fingers of her other hand walk.

Fargo frowned in thought for a moment and then felt the spiral of excitement inside him as he made a connection. "Walking and looking. You want me to go look for her," he said. Amanda nodded. "It could be too late," he said and she gave him a defiant glance.

She went to a corner of the room and picked up a leather traveling bag. She held it up to him and he thought again for a moment. "Bag. Arlene's bag?" he muttered.

Amanda shook her head impatiently and he gestured helplessly with his hands. She turned, pulled clothes from the dresser, and started to stuff them into the bag. She halted midway and stared at him, holding the bag up again.

"Clothes put into the bag," Fargo thought aloud, seeking connections, and once again he felt the sudden joining sweep through him. "Arlene had a bag. She packed a bag and took it with her." Amanda nodded and set the traveling bag down. "All right, I understand," Fargo said. "Arlene was running with her bag packed. She wanted to get away. She was really afraid but you don't know why."

Amanda nodded, her light brown hair tumbling.

Fargo frowned into space as he gave his own thoughts free rein. Amanda waited, watching him and he spoke his thoughts aloud for her. "Maybe Red Bull didn't take her at all. Maybe that was a conclusion everybody just came to, an assumption that might be very wrong." He brought his eyes back to Amanda. "Did you tell Kray this?" he asked and she answered with a negative shake of her head. "Why not?" he pressed.

Amanda clasped her arms around herself and went into the trembling motion again. "You're afraid of Kray, too," Fargo said and she nodded. "Has he ever done anything to you?"

Amanda pointed to Arlene's initial on the hairbrush again and then stretched her arms straight out as though she were pushing him away.

"Arlene stopped him. Arlene protected you," Fargo said.

Amanda nodded and again gestured for him to search for Arlene. She stopped, waited and he saw the insistence in her eyes, a sudden intensity as though she were trying to command him by sheer willpower.

"I can try," he said, his tone not offering much hope. "She carried a traveling bag full of clothes. Anything else? She take a horse?"

Amanda shook her head no and suddenly turned, went to the dresser, pulled a purple sash from a drawer, and tied it around her waist.

"She wore a sash," Fargo said, and Amanda nodded. "Same color?" Amanda nodded again and put the sash away. "You know which way she went?" Fargo asked.

Amanda lifted her arms and began to flap them to simulate the motion of a bird's wings. Fargo frowned back. "A bird," Fargo thought aloud. "What the hell does that mean?" Amanda waved her arms and made a circle with them as though she were holding some-

46

thing big. "Damn," Fargo swore as thoughts failed to connect. She began to simulate a bird's flight again. "A bird," he repeated. "No, a lot of birds," and Amanda nodded. "Birds flying," he said, thoughts coming together. "Birds flying. Where do birds fly? Jesus, birds flying south," he spit out and Amanda nodded. "She went south." Amanda's eyes agreed with him. "All right, I'll try to pick up her trail come morning," he said. Amanda took his hand, brought it to her face, and pressed it against her cheek. It was her gesture of gratitude, he realized, and it was echoed by the deep dark of her eyes. He smiled and pressed her hand in reply, and she turned and gestured to the large mattress. "You want me to stay?" he asked in surprise and she nodded. "You'd feel safer?" She nodded again.

His shrug was consent. His cot hadn't been all that comfortable and the two big mattresses could accommodate four. He put the Colt on the floor beside the edge of the mattress and Amanda turned out the lamp. The room was plunged into darkness that wasn't quite total, because the window let in a tint of moonlight. He shed his trousers, lay down on the one mattress, and saw her climb onto the one alongside as his eyes adjusted to the dim light. She lifted a sheet up, pulled the gray dress from herself, and slid under the sheet. She stayed distant as he lay back, his sheet only draped across his groin, and he saw her as she lay on her side, her eyes watching him.

"Good night, Amanda," he said softly. For a while she continued to take in his smoothly muscled body. Then she turned her back to him. Soon he heard the deep, steady breathing as she slept. He smiled as he closed his eyes and thought about how well she made herself understood. She hadn't been mute all her life, he wagered. He had seen the sign language of the deaf and she had used none of it, not even accidentally. But the sweet, silent Amanda had given him a lot to think about. He drew sleep around himself, aware that the night would end quickly enough.

The morning sun woke him when its first rays slanted in through the window and he sat up to see Amanda on the adjacent mattress, still modestly under the sheet but one bare shoulder and arm showing. She came awake as he rose, and she sat up. She held the sheet to her breasts, but he took in her beautifully rounded shoulders. "Come outside when you're dressed and show me where Arlene went when she ran," he said. "I don't want to cross through the house. Is there a back door?"

Amanda rose, keeping the sheet wrapped around her, stepped into the corridor with him, and pointed to a narrow door a few feet away. She waited till he slipped outside, and as she turned to go back to the room, he saw a flash of long, lovely calf at the bottom of the sheet. Outside, he hurried around the corner of the house to find himself at the lean-to and his room. He climbed in through the window as the sun rose over the distant hills. He washed and dressed and went out to the front room where Kray's woman had the coffeepot on the table. He had almost finished his mug when Amanda appeared, the splint broom in her hand. She hardly acknowledged his presence but when he went outside he found her behind him.

She motioned furtively to a long stand of forest, mostly black oak so far as he could tell. It spread out beyond a passage between two hillocks. Fargo pressed his hand to her arm, and she retreated back into the inn. He started to go to fetch the Ovaro but he halted in surprise as Captain Cogswell appeared. The captain was in the saddle with some twenty-five troopers behind. Kray walked along beside him as he moved from the barracks area and Fargo felt an alarm go off inside himself. "Real early patrol today?" he asked.

Cogswell's smile was made of satisfied anticipation. "No patrol," he said. "I'm going to wipe out one of their camps."

Fargo frowned at the man. "I thought you were going to wait for those twenty-five new men before you set things off," he said.

"No need for that. They'll be here, probably later today. A day or two won't matter. Red Bull will need a little time to realize what's happening. My new men will be here by then," the captain said.

Fargo's thoughts tumbled. He had to be careful not to say too much. He still had nothing but Amanda's contentions. "Anybody ever think Arlene maybe had an accident or just got herself lost?" he asked.

"She knew her way around. She wouldn't get lost," Kray snapped. "And I had men out searching for her."

"Yes, the captain mentioned that," Fargo remembered.

"And I told you that my search party, though much too long after, found Indian pony prints in the area she'd gone," Cogswell reminded him. Fargo nodded and digested the answers and allowed a small shrug.

"Guess you did all you could do," he said.

"Until now," Cogswell said. "Now I'm going to flush out that red-skinned weasel." He pumped one arm as he put his horse into a trot, and the squad fell in behind him. Fargo strode away to where the Ovaro was tethered, his lips a thin line. His search for Arlene's tracks would have to be put off. There was more immediate business at hand. He had to try and slow down the captain's plans. That had to come first.

Fargo saddled the pinto and swung onto the horse. He held himself back, keeping the horse at a trot as he left the inn. Kray was watching him, his darting eyes filled with suspicion. Fargo kept the pinto at a slow trot until he swung into the trees and then emerged a few hundred yards to go into a gallop. He rode up a hill and halted to find the captain's column and spotted the thin plume of dust heading toward the shallow valley thick with black oak and cottonwood. The second of the two camps he had detected lay in that valley, and Fargo again put the pinto into a gallop. He cut across a hill, down the other side, staying at the edge of the tree line to maintain his speed. The captain would keep his squad riding at a steady canter, he was certain. They'd only break into a charge when they were in sight of the Cheyenne camp.

Fargo's eyes narrowed. He estimated he could reach the Indian encampment some five minutes before the captain, perhaps ten if he was lucky. He kept the pinto galloping full-out as he plunged into the shallow dip of land. He counted on the unlikelihood that the Cheyenne had sentries posted at a small field encampment, but he was prepared to duck arrows. He let his nose guide him as he drew in deep breaths and finally picked up the odor of wood smoke and hides being dried. He turned the pinto through a passage in the cottonwoods, followed the odor, and soon glimpsed the tipis through the trees, not more than five or six clustered in a clearing. He saw the Cheyenne in the camp turn in alarm as they caught the sound of the Ovaro's galloping hooves.

Most were squaws. There were a half-dozen children and the rest were old men with but a few young bucks. The young bucks and old men dived for their bows as he charged into the camp and the squaws scattered, some scooping up children. Fargo yanked the pinto to a halt, flattened himself to avoid two arrows that sailed over his head and straightened up as he threw both arms into the air. He held his position of half-surrender, half-peace and saw the arrows poised on bowstrings to hurtle into him. "Soldiers come. Bluecoats," he shouted. The arrows stayed poised but the Cheyenne archers didn't release the bowstrings.

"They are coming now, to kill everyone. Many soldiers, too many," Fargo shouted. "You run or be killed."

He saw two of the younger men draw their bowstrings back, uncertainty on their faces, while an old man with a thin, ancient body clothed only in a breechclout stepped forward. "Why do you come here?" he asked.

Fargo made the sign for a long campfire story, one too long to tell at one sitting. "Run. They are near," he said and heard the murmur from some of the women. Two of them gathered children and began to hurry from the camp and Fargo watched the others as they began to follow. The young braves, faces still confused and uncertain, were the last to move but they, too, gathered their horses and began to flee. They all headed into the thickness of the forest behind the camp. They would scatter, there, he knew; the children were wise enough in the ways of survival to be silent. They'd scatter and flee in small, still groups of not more than two or three each, disappearing into the forest as if they were made of smoke.

They had believed him mainly because they could think of no reason why he would burst in on them to lie, he realized, and he took a moment to glance around the camp. Four elk hides were drying on fleshing racks and he spied stone bowls of dried meat and berries being ground into pemmican. He made a face as his ears picked up the sound of the horses. He wheeled the pinto in a tight circle and spurred the horse into the trees to his right and up a small incline. He halted at a spot that let him see down at the camp. The sound of hooves suddenly changed character.

The captain had caught sight of the camp and sent his squad into a full charge. Fargo watched him race into the camp, his troopers at his heels, carbines in hand, as Cogswell reined to a halt. "They've gone. Goddammit, they've gone," the captain swore. "Not long, either. Search the trees. Make a circle and search around the camp." The captain stayed in the center of the camp as his men rode off to search the perimeters, pushing through the trees and brush with the kind of noise and haste that would have make it impossible to find anyone who might have been there. In any case the Cheyenne were already far away and the braves were on their ponies, racing to the other camp to alert them.

Fargo waited till the search was ended and the men moved their horses back into the camp before he slowly sent the Ovaro down the slope. Captain Cogswell paused in his cursing to look up as Fargo came out of the trees, surprise filling his face. "What the hell are you doing here, Fargo?" the captain barked.

"I was riding up on the ridge and saw you and your men charging. I just came down to see for myself," Fargo said blandly.

"You won't see much. The damn savages ran. I don't know how they knew we were coming," Cogswell said.

"Ever hear of sentries?" Fargo inquired.

"We didn't see any damn sentries," Cogswell snapped.

"Chances are you won't see Cheyenne sentries," Fargo said.

The captain's mouth tightened. "Dammit to hell,"

he swore and barked orders to his men. "Destroy this place and everything in it," he said.

"That'll show them," Fargo remarked, drawing a sharp glare from the captain. He sat quietly and watched the troopers destroy tipis, hides, and everything else in the sparse camp. When they were finished the captain turned to him, his eyes narrowed. "Funny, you're being here right at this time, Fargo," he remarked.

"Coincidence. The world's full of them," Fargo said nonchalantly.

"There's another camp and I'm going to hit it. Maybe you'd like to ride along with us, Fargo," Cogswell said.

Fargo smiled inwardly. The offer had the continuing hint of suspicion in it. He didn't want to make Cogswell any more uneasy. He wanted to be able to reach the man. "Sure, I'd like that," Fargo said, also aware that there was not a lot of time left in the day for him to start tracking Arlene.

"Let's ride," Cogswell said, and Fargo drew up alongside him as the troop headed south. The captain returned to a slow canter. He knew enough not to tire the horses and men before they reached their destination, Fargo noted. But then that was pretty elementary military tactics. He rode in silence as the captain led his men across the rolling terrain and into the forestland where Fargo had pinpointed the other Cheyenne field camp. This time the captain spread his troopers out further as he proceeded through the forest until the open land came into sight. He didn't go into a charge but switched into a fast canter with his men stretched out in a horizontal line behind him. Fargo again smiled inwardly. Different tactics but the result would be the same, he grunted.

He drew the Colt from its holster as he burst into

the open with the captain. It was a nice touch, he smiled to himself. The Cheyenne camp was silent and empty. They'd had time to take their tipis down and make off with them, he saw, all their hides, too. Only two small fires and some hot stones in a pit marked the fact that there had been a camp there recently. That and two travois that had been left to one side.

"Damn them," the captain swore.

"Some other time," Fargo commented.

"You're goddamn right about that," Cogswell bit out as he spun his horse around and led the squad from the scene.

Fargo fell back, rode at the end of the column, and watched the day begin to slide toward dusk as they rode back. He hadn't bought a lot of time, yet anything that helped put off the start of a full-scale war was worth it. It had only been a stopgap act, he realized. It would take a lot more to prevent what seemed inevitable, given the captain's short-sighted determination. Then there was Red Bull. By morning, the Indian chief would know of the two raids. But as none of his people had been slain, he might not explode with rage. Not yet, at least, Fargo hoped.

It was all a precarious balancing act and he needed something to make the captain slow his headlong rush to incite an uprising. Perhaps finding out more about what had happened to Arlene would give him some ammunition. But that would have to wait till morning. Meanwhile the day was fading, and he reached Kray's Corners at the tail of the squad. He dismounted and saw Kray hurry over to Cogswell. The bitter anger in Kray's face reflected the captain's report.

Fargo took the pinto to the lean-to, gave the horse a quick brushing, and fed him oats he had purchased from the troop supply master.

When he strolled back to the front of the inn he saw Doc Schroder leaning against a hitching post and puffing on a pipe. " 'Evening," he called out. "Skipping supper?"

The army doctor smiled. "I'm letting Burton eat alone tonight. The captain's in a foul mood, but then you know about that, don't you?"

"Firsthand," Fargo said cheerfully.

"I imagine you viewed it as a blessing in disguise," Doc Schroder said.

"The Lord works in strange ways," Fargo said.

"He does indeed," the doctor smiled. "Good night, Fargo."

" 'Night," Fargo returned and strolled into the inn where Rosita served his meal at the big table. The stew again, second day but tasting even better than it had the first. He ate quickly, and when he finished Amanda appeared to clear away dishes. He whispered to her when she paused beside him. "I'll see about Arlene tomorrow," he said and her eyes nodded understanding. She had probably overheard the captain's conversation with Kray, he speculated.

When she went into the kitchen he rose and strolled outside to see the beefy-faced sergeant talking with a soldier posted as a sentry. The sergeant saw him, looked instantly uncomfortable, and hurried back to the barracks.

The night had stayed warm. Fargo sauntered out beyond the barracks and watched the half-moon hang in the black velvet sky. He saw a herd of whitetails move silently across a nearby slope, and their silent gracefulness made him think about Amanda. He let his eyes swing down to the handful of buildings and the double row of barracks and stables.

He was glad to see that Cogswell had posted a sentry. It was prudent military procedure. The captain

had been trained well enough. He was just inexplica-
bly pigheaded and inexperienced. Or maybe something more, Fargo reflected. His determination seemed
to hold something more than pigheadedness. Perhaps
he was being too influenced by Kray's thirst for vengeance. Fargo reflected a moment more and then put
aside further speculation as he walked back to the inn.
Only a small lamp burned low in the big front room.
He had started down the corridor toward his room
when he caught the movement at the opening of one
of the other corridors. He paused, hidden in the darkness against the wall, and saw the figure move down
the corridor with soft, stealthy steps. Kray, Fargo realized as the man passed a window where the dim
moonlight caught the side of his face. Why was he
sneaking around his own inn, Fargo wondered. As the
man disappeared down the corridor, Fargo moved
from the wall and followed.

As he entered the other corridor on equally silent
steps and crept along one wall toward the end he suddenly recognized the wide window at the very end of
the hall. Amanda's room was only a few feet from the
window. Fargo hurried his steps to reach the closed
door that marked her room. He heard a sudden thump
from inside and leaned his ear to the door. The voice
came through to him. "Dammit, stop running around,
you little bitch," Kray said in a raspy voice. Fargo
continued to keep his ear pressed to the door. "Look,
you be nice to me and I'll see Rosita lets up on you,"
Kray said. Fargo heard the quick movement of footsteps and then another curse. "Goddammit, stop that.
She ain't here to save your little ass now," Kray's
voice said. Fargo heard the sound of a lunge and another curse.

He closed his hand around the doorknob and turned
it, pushed the door open to see Kray trying to cut off

Amanda as she leaped lightly across the mattresses. Amanda saw him first, swerved past Kray's attempt to grab her, and ran across the room. Fargo felt her softness hit into his chest. Kray whirled around to stare at him.

"What the hell are you doing here?" Kray snarled.

"Just what I was going to ask you," Fargo said.

"I can go anywhere I want to go in this place," Kray said.

"I was invited," Fargo lied, and Amanda nodded vigorously.

"Well, I'm uninvitin' you," Kray said.

Fargo glanced down at Amanda. "You want me to go?" he asked. She shook her head, pointed to Kray and then at the door. "I believe the young lady wants you to leave," Fargo said.

"I'm going to teach you to mind your own goddamn business," Kray said and started toward him.

"Don't do anything stupid," Fargo said calmly. But Kray's eyes had stopped darting and were concentrated pinpoints of fury. Fargo motioned Amanda to step away from him, and she went to one side. Kray continued toward him, lips drawn back in a snarl of anger. Fargo tightened his shoulder muscles as he prepared for Kray's charge. The man had plainly let anger conquer common sense. Kray suddenly leaped forward, and Fargo started to bring up a whistling left hook when he saw Kray twist and grab hold of Amanda. He yanked her in front of him, and suddenly there was a hunting knife in his hand. A wicked-looking curved blade protruded from a bone hilt. Kray had the blade pressed against Amanda's throat.

"Drop your gun," he ordered. "No tricks or I'll cut her damn head off." The man's fury was out of hand. The incident was escalating more than Fargo had expected or wanted. He slowly lifted the Colt from its holster and let it slide to the floor. "Kick it over here," Kray said, and Fargo reached a foot out and sent the gun spinning almost to the man's feet. Fargo tightened his powerful leg muscles. He was ready as Kray did just what he expected. The man reached down to pick up the gun. To do so, he had to pull the knife away from Amanda's throat. Fargo flung himself forward in a hurtling dive that slammed him into Kray just as the man's hand started to close around the gun. "Shit," Kray swore as he fell backward, and the revolver skittered from his fingertips.

Fargo landed half atop him and saw Kray try to bring the hunting knife around in a short arc. Kray's arm came down sideways, but Fargo managed to curl his fingers around the man's wrist. He bore down hard, using the powerful muscles of his shoulders, and Kray's hand went backward. When his arm followed he let out a sharp gasp of pain, and the knife dropped from his hand. Fargo released his grip and brought a short, hard right around that hit Kray against the side of the jaw. Kray rolled across the floor, stopped himself, and started to get to his feet. Fargo's left caught him flash on the point of the jaw, and he went down on his back and lay still.

Fargo bent over, picked up the Colt and the knife, and handed the blade to Amanda. "Put it away with your things. It might come in handy sometime," he told her and she took the weapon from his hand. He heard Kray groan and saw the man lift his head. His eyes fluttered and finally came open.

Fargo closed a hand around Kray's shirtfront and lifted him to his feet. "You touch this girl again and there won't be room enough for you to hide west of the Mississippi," he said and flung the man against the wall.

Kray, the fight gone out of him, held onto sullen threats. "I won't be forgetting this, Fargo," he muttered.

"Make sure you don't," Fargo said. Kray edged to the door, yanked it open, and slid from the room. Fargo took a step forward and pushed the door shut with one foot. Kray had shown himself to be more vicious than he'd expected, and Fargo wondered if the three troopers had hired the knife-wielding attacker. He hadn't entirely ruled out Kray in the first place. Now he wouldn't rule him out at all. He turned as Amanda came to him, once again took his hand, and pressed it to her cheek. But this time she leaned against him for a long moment and he smelled the sweet womanliness of her.

She stepped back, her brown eyes round and grave, and she gestured to the mattress again with a sweep of her hand. "You want me to stay again?" he asked. She nodded, and he smiled and ran his hand over the light brown hair. "I'll be obliged," he said and waited for a smile but there was only the round, grave eyes and the seriousness of her lovely face. She turned and put out the lamp. He sat down in the darkness, shed his clothes, and stretched out on the mattress with the sheet pulled over his groin. The dark turned a shade lighter as his eyes grew accustomed to the dim moonlight that barely entered the room, and he saw Amanda on the mattress beside him. She pulled the dress from herself before sliding under the sheet this time, and he glimpsed the dark silhouette of the up-turned sweep of her breasts, their outline fuller than he'd expected.

She drew the sheet over herself as she lay on her side, and he saw her eyes moving across his body until finally she closed them and fell asleep. He turned on his side and did the same, more certain than ever that this was a place where nothing was quite what it seemed to be, except for hate and death.

4

He woke with the morning and immediately felt the warmth on his arm. It was not the new sun but Amanda's hand resting across his upper arm. He turned his head and saw that she was still asleep. The sheet was rolled down enough so that the lovely, soft swell of her breasts rose over the top edge. He moved quietly, slid her hand from his arm, and swung from the mattress to don only trousers. She was still asleep when he tiptoed out of the room and made his way back to his own room, where he washed and dressed.

The enameled coffeepot was on the big table when he went outside. He poured a mug of coffee for himself, finished it, and stepped from the inn. He saw Kray opening the doors of the trading post, and when Kray saw him he came over, his tight-skinned face made of sheepishness. "Sorry about last night," Kray said. "I had a few drinks and I guess I let them go to my head. I'm glad you stopped me from doing something I'd have been sorry about today."

"That makes two of us," Fargo said.

"No hard feelings," Kray offered and let the sheepishness color his smile.

"That's good," Fargo said evenly. Kray offered another smile and hurried back to the trading post. Fargo grunted silently. A wolf in sheep's clothing. The man was smart enough not to carry on something that might not sit well with the captain. Fargo saw Doc

Schroder come into sight and then Cogswell with an aide bringing him his mount. "More reconnoitering today?" Fargo asked.

"That's right. I know there's another camp not far away. Red Bull has had his squaws out getting ready for winter, tanning plenty of skins and furs," the captain said.

"Your twenty-five new men arrive?" Fargo questioned.

"No. I expect they'll show today sometime," the captain said. Fargo stepped back as a squad of twenty troopers rode up. Cogswell swung onto his mount and led his men away. Fargo started to walk to the Ovaro, then paused before the doctor.

"Got a question for you, Doc," he said. "The young girl, Amanda, you have any chance to watch her?"

"Yes, I have."

"You think she always was a mute?" Fargo queried.

The doctor thought for a moment. "No, I don't think so. I've watched the way she makes herself understood, when she wants to, that is. She's developed her own sign language."

"Pretty much what I've been thinking," Fargo said. "Just wanted some expert opinion. See you around, Doc." He strode on and saddled the Ovaro. This time he didn't take off after the captain but followed the path through the two hillsides where Amanda said Arlene had gone. He kept the horse at a slow walk when he reached the black oak, his practiced eyes searching the forest floor. Ordinarily he'd have had little trouble picking up a single set of footprints, but a fair amount of time had gone by. There'd been no heavy rains since Arlene had left the inn, but the night winds had a way of covering up prints. Yet this was not a heavily traveled forest, he noted with gratitude. He saw no hoof marks, no clusters of footprints that would mean trappers, no low, young twigs snapped off that would indicate print-obliterating herds of deer and elk.

He walked the horse in short, zigzag patterns that let him cover the forest in wide swaths. It was slow and painstaking work and he had searched for more than two hours when he finally spied the marks he sought, a lone set of footprints cutting across a soft piece of forest where an underground stream flowed. He followed the tracks, losing them occasionally, but quickly picking them up again. Arlene had walked pretty much in a straight line, he saw, and he found a place where she had halted to rest beside a dry log. When the prints appeared again, he followed them until he came to a long, dense growth of blackberry whose thorny brambles extended beyond sight in both directions.

She had walked back and forth to find a way around them, realizing there was none, had plunged through. He did the same, walking the horse carefully, and his eyes spotted the tiny, torn bits of dress fabric clinging in individual pieces to the brambles in various places. When he had pushed his way through the thorny bushes to the other side he picked up her footprints again. She had a good sense of direction, he noted. She headed south with hardly any wandering away. He'd gone perhaps another hour when the footsteps halted their steady trail and darted to the right. Then they went left and Fargo frowned as he reined to a halt. Another set of prints went north, deeper than those he'd been following. She had started running. He saw the marks that converged after her, unshod Indian pony prints, and the smooth prints of deerskin moccasins.

Fargo dismounted, followed on foot, and halted where her prints were half obscured by the moccasin prints. He knelt down on one knee and read the signs on the ground as other men read a book. A lone set of pony prints came in from the left, then another from the right and both sets finally moved away together. He found Arlene's footprints again, steps deeper and sometimes dragged. She had been taken, tied, and pulled along after the horses in the typical fashion of Indians' captives. Fargo swung onto the pinto and followed the trail until he saw where another four ponies had joined the first two. The trail moved out of the forest and onto partly open land, and Fargo drew to a halt, a frown on his forehead.

He could always return to pick up the trail, but there were other questions he wanted answered first, and he rode back to the spot in the forest where Arlene had been seized. Dropping to the ground again, he searched the surrounding bushes and came upon the bag. It had been tossed into the brush. Most of the contents had spilled out. He knelt and pored through the blouses, slips, and half-slips, combs, and water canteen and hair clips. He found a Bible and a small, pocket-size tintype in a simple wood frame, the name *Arlene* written across the bottom. He took a moment to study the photo and saw a young woman with wide-spaced eyes, a face more pleasant than pretty, with brown hair braided and worn tightly around her face. He put the tintype in his pocket as he rose to his feet. Arlene had a face as well as a name, now. But he had learned more than that.

Amanda had been very right. Arlene had not simply been running. She had been leaving, taking her personal things with her. She had no intention of returning. And she most definitely hadn't gone out for a walk in the woods. Kray had known that, Fargo wagered. He must have seen that her things were missing as well as she. Yet he'd lied to Cogswell about her having gone out for a walk. Why, Fargo frowned.

Because he didn't want to admit she had run away? It was an answer he couldn't dismiss but couldn't really accept, either. Maybe he thought that was the best way to get Cogswell to look for her. Fargo drew his lips back, dissatisfied with this explanation as well. But whatever the reason, he was convinced Kray knew and had lied about it.

The man had been right about only one thing; the Cheyenne taking her. That had probably been an educated guess. He wound up having lied about Arlene yet being right. Dammit, nothing was cut-and-dried here, Fargo decided as he gathered up the girl's things, stuffed everything except the tintype back into the traveling bag, and tied the bag onto the back of his saddle. He climbed onto the pinto and began to follow the trail of the Indian ponies. He stayed on the trail as it finally led out of the forest onto open low hills with clusters of tree cover. He was continuing after the prints when he spotted six near-naked riders. A Cheyenne hunting party, he saw instantly and had a moment to push himself into a cluster of hawthorn.

They were riding at a fast canter, directly over the trail he had intended to follow. They were thoroughly obliterating it, he knew, not on purpose, but the end result was the same. He stayed in the hawthorn till they had gone their way. When he backed away from the wide, thick cover he turned the pinto and started back toward Kray's Corners, now a fair-sized ride. His thoughts turned slowly in his mind as he rode. He had enough to go to Cogswell and buy some more time, get the man to pull back a little in his haste to confront the Cheyenne chief. He thought about Kray's lies about Arlene. There were hidden currents at work he couldn't decipher yet. Perhaps Amanda could shed some light on that. He kept a steady pace but the night had descended when he reached Kray's Corners.

He unsaddled the Ovaro, left Arlene's bag with the saddle, covered it with a saddle blanket, and walked to the inn. He had decided to let the captain have his dinner before paying him a visit. He found Amanda in the front room when he entered, standing by a clay pot on the table, a ladle in her hand.

Her round, brown eyes seemed to hold relief when she saw him enter. He sat down at the table, and she served him pieces of cut-up boiling hen in a gravy with hard bread on the side; he realized he was very hungry when he took the first bite. He was about to talk to her when Kray entered. The man was still wearing his mask of contrition, Fargo noted, his friendliness entirely too unctuous. "Have a good day?" Kray asked him.

"I think so. Did a good piece of exploring," Fargo said. "The captain find Red Bull?"

"No, but he located that other Cheyenne hunting camp," Kray said. "He plans to hit it tomorrow. Maybe you'd like to ride with him," Kray added, and Fargo smiled at the oblique challenge.

"Maybe," Fargo smiled. "The captain's twenty-five new men arrive?"

"No," Kray said and walked from the room with a friendly wave. Fargo glanced across the table to see Amanda's waiting eyes. He also caught a glimpse of Rosita's shadow by the kitchen door.

"Later," he murmured, and Amanda's eyes told him she understood. He finished the meal, went outside, retrieved the small traveling bag from the Ovaro's saddle, and walked into the barracks area. He saw the lamplight in the window of Cogswell's quarters, and the door was opened to his knock. The captain stared at him, surprise in his face. His uniform collar was still buttoned. Cogswell's glance went down to the traveling bag.

"Come to say good-bye?" the officer inquired.

"Not exactly," Fargo said, and Cogswell motioned for him to step inside. The small office was as neat as its occupant, two straightbacked chairs, a small desk, and not a piece of paper out of place. Fargo set the bag down, took the tintype from his pocket, and placed it on the desk in front of the captain. "Found this in the woods," he said.

"Arlene Kelly," Cogswell said after a moment.

"Her picture. No doubt very important to her," Fargo said, reached down and put the small traveling bag on the desk. "This was nearby. Her traveling bag. All her personal belongings in it, clothes, extra shoes, and her Bible." Cogswell looked at him, his glance inquiring. "She wasn't out for a walk," Fargo said. "She was running away."

"Aren't you jumping to conclusions?" Cogswell said.

"No. Besides, that's what Amanda told me," Fargo said.

The captain raised one eyebrow quizzically. "Amanda told you?"

"All right, that's what she made me understand," Fargo said with a flash of irritation. "This is proof of it. A young woman doesn't go for a walk in the woods with all her personal possessions. She was running away, dammit. Kray lied to you about her going for a stroll."

The captain studied the tintype for a moment and then handed it back to Fargo. "You found these things. You did a better job than my men, but then you must have seen the Cheyenne pony prints," he said.

"I saw them," Fargo admitted. "They came upon her and took her. That much is right."

"That's all that matters, isn't it?" the captain said with a note of condescension in his voice.

"No. Maybe a lot more matters," Fargo frowned.

"Such as?" Cogswell queried.

"Finding out why she was running away. Finding out why Kray lied to you about her going for a stroll. Maybe those things are important," Fargo said.

The captain's tone stayed condescending. "You can't really mean that," he said.

"I sure as hell do mean it. I'd think you'd want to find out why Kray lied to you," Fargo returned.

"Look, my dear fellow, I don't care about any personal arguments she might have had with Desmond Kray. I don't care what might have prompted her to go off in a huff, perhaps. She might make a practice of it," Cogswell said.

"Then why didn't he tell you that?" Fargo pressed.

"Perhaps he was embarrassed, ashamed to tell me she ran away. Or perhaps he really did think she'd gone for a walk. Perhaps he still does think that. You've no proof otherwise," the captain said, and Fargo felt his lips tighten at that truth. "The important thing is that the Cheyenne did take her. That's the one, single fact that I care about," Cogswell said.

"Why?" Fargo frowned.

"Because it's my duty to care about that, not about personal quarrels," Cogswell said.

Fargo peered at the captain. There was something self-serving about the man's loftiness. "Bullshit," Fargo snapped out and saw Cogswell's face tighten. "That's all you want to care about," Fargo said. "It's your perfect excuse."

"You call it excuse. I call it opportunity. Army politics sent me out to this goddamn hellhole but I'm not going to be stuck here the way others have been. When I wipe out a major force of hostiles they'll come crawling to me. I'll be able to write my own ticket out of here," Cogswell said.

"And you're willing to sacrifice God knows how many lives for your ambition," Fargo said. "That's a new low, I'd say."

"I'm going to protect the people of this territory and that'll be a new high," Cogswell returned. "I'd advise you to stay out of my way, Fargo. I know my duty and I'll do it."

"You know your ambition, that's all you know," Fargo said angrily as he took the traveling bag and strode from the office. He was still wrapped in anger as he hurried from the barracks area, and he didn't see the figure in the shadows until the voice spoke to him.

"Have a less than pleasant visit with the captain?" the voice asked, and Fargo halted to see Doc Schroder step from the darker shadows.

"Bull's eye," Fargo said.

"The captain can be a difficult man," the army doctor said.

"The captain's a damn fool, self-centered, and full of blind ambition, and they're the worst kind," Fargo spat out. "He's going to get a hell of a lot of people killed."

"I hope you're wrong about that," Schroder said.

"Keep hoping," Fargo grunted. "I understand his new men didn't arrive today."

"That's right," the doctor said.

"I'm wondering if there are any new men or if that was something he just threw out at me," Fargo said.

"No, there are twenty-five new men due. I saw the approved requisition. An assistant for me is supposed to be with them," Doc Schroder told him.

"Let's be grateful for small favors," Fargo said. "See you tomorrow, Doc." He strode on and went into the inn where a candle burned to give a dim and fitful light in the large front room. The reason for the captain's determination to risk an uprising was out in the open now. Maybe the man even believed he could wipe out Red Bull. But his personal ambition was paramount. He hadn't lied about that. Which left Desmond Kray. He had lied about Arlene going for a stroll. But why? Because of the reasons Cogswell had suggested? Or had he other reasons?

Fargo halted at the end of the corridor, at the closed door to Amanda's room, and knocked softly. She answered in moments, clothed in an off-white nightgown. It was modestly high-necked and knee-length, but the material was a light cotton that rested against the shapely contours of her figure. She closed the door as he entered and handed the bag to her. He saw the instant recognition leap into her eyes when she saw it. She gazed at him, the question hanging in the wide, brown orbs. "The Cheyenne have her," Fargo said with a nod. She took the bag and set it down in the corner, and when she returned to him he put his hands on her shoulders. "Arlene had a reason to run away. I want you to think hard, Amanda. Why did she run? Why was she afraid?"

Amanda sank down on the edge of the mattress, her legs held against each other as she shrugged helplessly.

"You can't think of any reason? You can't guess at one?" he questioned and she again said no with her eyes. He saw the helpless frustration in her eyes, sank down beside her, and let his own thoughts pull what little he knew together. Arlene had worked for Kray for years and she hadn't run. Then suddenly she had decided to flee. Something had happened to make her do it, something new, something she had learned. The captain was away on a three-day patrol and she was too frightened to wait for his return. He was becoming more and more certain that it had something to do with Desmond Kray, and if it did, the man knew very well why she had run. Yet that didn't fit with the way he prodded Cogswell to wipe out Red Bull for taking Arlene.

Guilt might explain that for some men, but he didn't read Desmond Kray as harboring much of a conscience. He pushed away further musings. They were useless without something more to go on. He pushed to his feet.

"I don't know what's really happened to Arlene by now. But if she's alive maybe she's the one that can answer the questions. I'll try to find out both things," he said to Amanda. "There's another trail I might be able to pick up." She nodded, stood up with a quick, fluid motion, and gestured to the mattress again with a sweep of her arm. "You want me to stay the night again," he said and she answered with a quick, short nod. She spun away and turned off the lamp. The room again plunged into near pitch black until his eyes adjusted. Then the faint moonlight let him see her shadowy figure settling onto the adjoining mattress.

He undressed, aware of her eyes on him, and lay down with the sheet only flung across his groin. He glanced across at Amanda. She was closer than she'd been on the other nights, within easy arm's reach, lying on her side, her eyes closed. He let her own eyelids close when suddenly he felt her hand against his shoulder. He turned his head to look at her. Her eyes stayed closed and he wasn't sure if she was half-asleep or not. But her hand stayed on his shoulder, unmoving, childlike, and he pulled his eyes closed again and went to sleep.

When he woke with the morning sun her hand was still on his shoulder and she was still on her side asleep, but she had come closer, only inches from him, now. The loose neck of the nightgown showed the smooth line of the side of her left breast, more fullness to it than he'd imagined. Sliding from under her hand, which fell limply onto the mattress, he rose and used the washbasin to scrub. He was half dressed when she woke. He heard her stir and sit up and rub sleep from her eyes and come to focus on him. He stepped to the edge of the mattress and put one hand against her hair. "I'll be going, now," he said, and suddenly her arms were wrapped tightly around his legs and she clung there for a moment before just as suddenly letting go. He smiled down at her serious face. It had been another of her ways to express herself. Caring and gratitude were in the gesture.

He stepped to the door and hurried from the room. He had already learned that Amanda could communicate thoughts despite her silence. Now he knew she could communicate feelings, too, and he made a mental note to speak to Doc Schroder more about her. Outside, he blinked for a moment in the morning brightness and looked down the line of the stables where the troopers had their mounts out for morning grooming. He paused, staring again, and felt a frown slide across his brow. There weren't more than twenty-five horses being brushed, and he stepped to the nearest trooper with a sponge in one hand. "Where's the rest of the squad, soldier?" he asked.

"With the captain. They left at dawn," the trooper said.

"Shit," Fargo swore as he spun on his heel and ran to the lean-to and the Ovaro. He flung his saddle on the horse. Minutes later he was galloping away from the line of barracks. His eyes swept the ground and quickly picked up the trail of the squad. That was easy enough to follow, but they had been riding hard, he saw, and they had over an hour's start on him. He kept the pinto in a fast canter for most of the way, following the trails across three low hills and then through a thin patch of red ash and serviceberry. Another low hillock crested before him when he emerged. Suddenly the sound of rifle fire erupted. "Goddamn," Fargo flung out as he put the Ovaro into a full gallop.

He raced up the hillock, cresting the top as the rifle fire continued. He was charging down the other side when the shooting died away just past a line of hackberry. His lips drawn back in disgust, his mind already painting the picture he'd find, he raced through the trees and into the Cheyenne camp. He skidded the Ovaro to a halt and the picture that had been painted in his mind became sickeningly real. The small camp was strewn with bodies, mostly squaws and naked children with a few old men and three young boys. Most of the bodies were dead from gunfire but a few had been bayoneted, he saw. Some of the troops were still beating the nearby brush while the rest sat their horses behind Cogswell. He saw the captain look at him with surprise.

"You have an unexpected way of turning up, don't you, Fargo," Cogswell commented.

Fargo walked the Ovaro forward through the littered camp grounds. Most of the Indian weapons were bows and lances, he noted, though he did see three carbines scattered on the ground. He halted in front of Cogswell. "You stupid bastard," he muttered tightly.

"Watch your tongue, mister," Cogswell flared. "Insulting an officer of the United States Cavalry is an offence."

"Excuse me. I sure as shit wouldn't want to do that. Murdering a bunch of squaws and kids is all right, I take it," Fargo bit out.

"Don't tell me you're bothered by that. Or haven't

you ever seen settler's women after an Indian raid?"
Cogswell asked disdainfully.

"I've seen them. I thought we were supposed to be a little more civilized," Fargo said. "But that's not really what's bothering me. It's your stinking, selfish blindness. You couldn't even wait for your reinforcements to get here before sticking everybody's neck out on the line."

"I know exactly what I'm doing, Fargo," the captain said.

"So do I," Fargo snapped bitterly as he wheeled the Ovaro around. He saw the beefy-faced sergeant and the other two troopers and reined up in front of them. "You boys must really have enjoyed this," he said, and they looked away with more discomfort then he had expected.

"I'll thank you not to harass my men," Cogswell called out. Fargo saw the three troopers exchange glances, sudden fear in their eyes, but he decided again to say nothing. More than ever, the settlers of the territory would need every gun that could protect them. Besides, the three troopers might pay for trying to rape the Cheyenne girl in ways they never imagined. But that Cheyenne girl had assumed a new importance. She might prove the one way he could reach the warrior chief. Fargo rode the Ovaro away from the death-stained camp without a glance back.

He was faced with picking up old tracks again, but Arlene's had been older and he rode back toward Kray's Corners. When he neared the buildings he saw the sun dropping across the distant sky. There'd be no day left to reach the area where he had saved the Cheyenne girl. That would have to wait for morning. He turned the horse and rode back to Kray's Corners.

Amanda was sweeping outside the inn when he arrived, and her brown orbs were filled with instant questions. "Tonight," he said as he passed her and saw Desmond Kray at the door of his trading post. Fargo unsaddled the pinto as the day moved to an end. He watched two Conestogas arrive and halt before the trading post. They disgorged at least five families, who picked up fresh supplies from Kray and were loaded and ready to roll when the captain arrived with his squad. Fargo watched him pause to talk to the settlers and waited until the wagons rolled away and Cogswell dismounted. "That wasn't much of a warning about Indian trouble," Fargo said.

"It was enough. They're heading north and they'll be well on their way before Red Bull decides what he's going to do about striking back," the captain said.

"He already knows what happened today and he's already made his plans for striking back," Fargo said.

"Good, because I'm going to be out there ready for him," Cogswell said, and Kray came up to stroll back to his quarters with him. Fargo turned away as he heard the captain telling what he'd done, with relish, to Kray's chortling approval. He went into the front room of the inn, where Rosita served him a meal of buffalo strips smothered in a hot sauce and he washed it down with plenty of water. He waited outside for a spell when he finished, let the woman close down the inn except for the lone candle, and saw Kray return, his steps a little unsteady, from the barracks area. Fargo felt the grim anger inside him. Celebrating too early was always an invitation to disaster.

He straightened up, went inside, and silently moved down the corridor to Amanda's room. She opened the door at his knock. She had the thin cotton nightdress on again and she listened gravely as he told her what had stopped him from going after Arlene. "Maybe tomorrow, Amanda," he said. "But stopping a war is first."

She nodded, lifted the hairbrush with Arlene's name on it, and held it up to him. "Arlene can stop it?" he asked. And she said no with a shake of her head. She held the brush up again and pointed to Arlene's name, then held up her forefinger. "Find Arlene first?" he said and she nodded. He put his arm around her shoulders, drew her to him, and felt the warmth of her. "I can't promise that," he said. "We don't know if Red Bull has her or if she's alive. First things first. I'll try to find her as soon as I can."

She stepped back and put the brush on the dresser. Her face was serious, and he searched the wide, brown eyes. They seemed to say that she accepted his answer, but unhappily. She gestured to the mattress again and he agreed by starting to unbutton his shirt. She waited till he had it off before she turned the lamp out. He finished undressing and stretched out on the mattress as the moon sent its weak light into the darkness. He saw Amanda lie down, but this time she was closer than ever before and as she turned on her side her head came against his shoulder. He found himself wondering and decided to turn and bring his arms around her as she lay close. Her eyes grew rounder and she twisted away at once, turned, and looked at him from the center of the other mattress.

"All right," he said gently. "I understand." He reached one arm out to her. "Come back." She moved toward him, half rolled and half turned, and yet it wound up a graceful motion and she settled down against him again, her head resting against his shoulder, and he saw the soft curve of one breast over the loose neckline of the nightdress. Once again silent, Amanda had made herself understood. She had told him she had grown closer to him, enough to want to touch him, come against him in a kind of silent sharing. But she wasn't ready for more. He heard her fall asleep against him. One arm came to lie across his chest, and he wondered as he let himself fall asleep if silent Amanda would ever be ready for more, or were her senses as completely locked away as her speech.

5

When Fargo woke with the new day Amanda's arm was still across his chest and her head tight against his shoulder. The light cotton nightdress had pulled up enough for him to see one slender and very lovely leg with a long calf and a rounded knee. He slid from under her arm. This time she woke and he felt her eyes watch him as he washed and drew on trousers. She was sitting up when he turned to her, and she pushed to her feet and was against him in three quick steps, her arms around his waist, her body pressed against him, warm and soft, and he felt the pressure of her breasts through the thin cotton garment. He pulled back to look at her and once again he saw only a wide-eyed, childlike seriousness in the dark brown orbs.

"I'll be careful," he said. "If I don't come back tonight, don't worry." But he saw the fear leap into her face. "You want me to try and find Arlene, don't you?" he asked, and she let the fear slide away. "That may take time." Amanda nodded in understanding, dropped to her knees, and put her palms together in the act of prayer. "Right, you pray for me, for a lot of people," he said, and she pushed to her feet and walked to the door with him. He left wondering if she had any idea how, in her silent, childlike way, she radiated a very womanly sensuality.

Outside, he saddled the Ovaro and had just finished

when he heard the troop riding out and he walked the horse around the corner of the barracks where the rest of the troop were beginning their chores. "He took twenty-five men, if that's what you're trying to figure out," Doc Schroder's voice said behind him, and he turned to see the army doctor stroll up. "The captain's hoping Red Bull will have at least some of his bucks out hunting for revenge. He figures to hit them whenever he sees them. Sight, pursue, and destroy, to use his words."

"That's right out of the field tactics textbook, I'd say," Fargo sniffed as he climbed onto the Ovaro. "Only the Cheyenne have their own textbook and Cogswell never read that." He waved back at the army doctor as he rode away, turned, and crested a low hill to turn southward. He'd only ridden a quarter mile when he spotted the patrol. Cogswell was in the lead, and Fargo paused to count some twenty-five troopers. They were heading south, also, but Fargo turned into the highland and moved along a ridge line, his eyes sweeping the ground.

He slowed as he spied the set of unshod hoofprints, not more than an hour old. Six horses, he guessed, and they were moving quickly. His glance went down across the terrain below and saw the long dip of land that stretched for some miles, plenty of rock and tree cover on both sides of it. He also saw the plume of dust that was the captain and his squad heading for the low stretch. The Indian ponies had also headed that way, he observed, and he put the Ovaro into a canter as he swung in behind a line of black oak. Making a quick appraisal of the terrain, he rode toward a cluster of low rocks that lay below the line of oak but above the dip of land. He slowed when he spotted another set of unshod pony tracks. More, this time, at least a dozen.

They led through the oak and downward and he followed, moving carefully now, his eyes searching the land below, traveling along the line of low boulders that bordered the nearest side of the low dip of land. Suddenly he saw the six bronzed horsemen riding single-file through the flatland, moving toward the plume of dust that marked the captain and his column. The plume was larger and closer now, heading into the shallow stretch of land. He knew the Cheyenne had to have seen it also, and he took his eyes away from the six riders. They had made the first set of prints he had seen, he decided. His eyes moved across the line of low boulders again. They came to a halt suddenly where a taller rock jutted upward and behind it he saw the band of Cheyenne, huddled together, waiting. He'd been right, at least a dozen, he grunted.

They'd stay exactly where they were, he knew, and he turned the Ovaro in the trees and put the horse into a fast canter toward the plume of dust. But his lips pulled back in a grimace. The captain had already moved into the shallow dip of land and Fargo saw the six Cheyenne still moving leisurely toward the column. As he watched, they came to a halt and Fargo saw the column come into sight. The captain had his men riding at a trot but when he saw the six Cheyenne in front of him he raised his arm and brought it down in a sharp pumping motion and the column went into a charging full gallop at once.

Fargo's eyes went to the six bronzed horsemen. They wheeled their sturdy ponies, first one way then the other. They seemed to be surprised and frightened, and then they gathered themselves and fled back down the shallow dip of land. "Jesus," Fargo spit out aloud. It was a performance so good they might have been taking acting classes. And now they were fleeing and the captain and his troopers were closing ground on them. Fargo spun the Ovaro around, still staying in the trees, and raced back the way he'd come. He reached the place just above the tall boulder where the other Cheyenne waited and yanked the big Sharps from its saddle case as he drew to a halt. Cogswell, hot in pursuit of the six fleeing Cheyenne, was almost at the tall boulder.

The Cheyenne's first strike out of the ambush would do the most damage, taking the column completely by surprise while the six fleeing Cheyenne would whirl and strike from in front. Seconds counted now, the precious seconds that would give the column a chance to take cover and avoid being caught completely and defenselessly by surprise. He raised the rifle to fire into the air to send the alarm when he paused and brought the gun around to the horsemen behind the boulder. He'd kill four birds with one stone, he realized. He'd sound the alarm, break up the main punch of the ambush, bring down at least two Cheyenne, and throw confusion into the rest. The Cheyenne, like all Indians, abhorred not knowing who or how many they faced.

The Cheyenne were starting to come out from beyond the boulder when he took aim, fired, and saw a short-legged form fly sideways from his pony. Another shot took down a young buck with a beaded wristband, and Fargo paused to throw a glance down into the shallow stretch of land. The captain had reined to a halt. Fargo heard him bark orders at his men, saw the troopers spur their horses into the trees and rocks along the other side. The Cheyenne were racing down the slope now, firing mostly arrows, but he heard a few shots and he took aim again. He fired two more shots and saw two of the riders topple from their ponies. Four of the attacking Cheyenne veered off and looked up at the trees, uncertainty on their broad faces. The six decoys were attacking and the others continued to the attack, but the force of the ambush had been broken. The troopers were firing back and Fargo saw another of the Cheyenne go down. He also glimpsed three troopers hit the ground with arrows sticking out from them.

Fargo raced the Ovaro a half-dozen yards to his left, still keeping to the trees, and fired off another round, this time bringing down only one of the attackers. But he saw the Cheyenne peer up into the treeline again, and suddenly one of them shouted, waving an arm, and the others spun their ponies and raced after him down along the stretch of land where it narrowed before widening again. The ambush had failed and they had broken off further attack, unwilling to be caught in a counterambush. Fargo reloaded the big Sharps and returned it to the saddle holster. It was over. But only for this one incident.

He pushed from inside the trees and walked the Ovaro down the slope to where the troopers were gathering themselves. Cogswell looked up as Fargo came down the slope and reined to a halt. He nodded, a slightly grudging appreciation in his voice.

"Sometimes you do pick a good moment to show up," he said.

"Looks that way," Fargo replied.

"Another coincidence?" Cogswell said.

"Not this time. I saw it coming together," Fargo said. "You lose anybody?"

"No. Three men wounded, none seriously," the captain said. "What did you mean about seeing it coming together?"

"Saw the six Cheyenne and was pretty damn sure you'd do just what you did, go chasing after them," Fargo said.

"Now just hold on. I'm not the first man to be tricked into an ambush," Cogswell protested.

"Only you wouldn't have been tricked into this one if you knew what you were doing. If you knew the Cheyenne you'd have seen those six for what they were—bait," Fargo said.

"How would I've seen that?" Cogswell frowned.

"By realizing they had to see your dust cloud, which meant they could have slipped away anytime. But they didn't. They let you come upon them. Someone who knows the Cheyenne would've smelled a rat right then. Instead, you took the bait, hook, line, and sinker."

"It's possible I underestimated their deviousness," the captain conceded.

"You're underestimating a lot more than deviousness," Fargo snorted.

"I'll force him into open combat. That's all I'll need," the captain said.

Fargo turned away as Cogswell went over to where his wounded men were being given first aid. He waited until the captain returned. "They can ride until we go back," Cogswell said. "For now we're going on for a while. Red Bull will have his scouts watching. I want him to see that his attack won't send us scurrying home." He swung into the saddle and motioned his men forward with a wave. He continued southward and Fargo decided to ride along for a few miles further before turning off. The captain held the pace to a slow trot in deference to the wounded men. They had gone for perhaps another mile when they crested a low rise and Fargo saw the flock of slow-wheeling forms clouding the air just beyond a second hillside. Cogswell halted the column as Fargo came alongside him.

"Buzzards," Fargo said. "Whatever it is it's drawn a damn lot of them."

Cogswell frowned at the birds as they wheeled and swooped down out of sight while others flew up into view. "I don't know of any settlers in this area," he said.

Fargo spurred the Ovaro forward. "I'll go have a look," he said and held the horse in a fast trot up the hillside. He had ridden halfway up the slope when the odor came to his nostrils, sickeningly sweet yet pungent, and he swore silently. It was an odor he had smelled before, too often, an odor once smelled never forgotten. He slowed the Ovaro as he reached the top of the hill and he stared down at a flat square of land. He stared down at it for a long moment, his eyes moving slowly over the bodies that lay strewn across the ground. Some were nearly naked, some mutilated, and all covered with the dried blood from the punctures of arrowheads.

The mutilation was being carried out by the horde of ripping, tearing beaks, their featherless, naked red heads somehow appropriately obscene, their huge grayish-black wings folding and unfolding like movable shrouds. They were the final, crowning blasphemy, and he drew the Colt and fired two shots into the middle of them. The vultures rose at once, sweeping skyward on their wide wings. Fargo gazed down at Cogswell and gestured to him. The captain left his troop and cantered up the hillside. He drew up alongside Fargo, and his face drained of color as he stared down at the scene below. Fargo watched the man's stare linger on the blue-and-gold-striped uniforms that littered the ground. "Don't bother counting," he said. "There'll be twenty-five."

Cogswell's lips worked soundlessly for a long moment. "My God. My God," the words finally came. "That savage, murdering bastard."

"That savage, murdering bastard has answered your

savage, murdering trip to the hunting camp," Fargo said. "It's only his first answer."

The captain met Fargo's eyes and turned away after a moment to beckon his troop up the hill. "We'll have to sort out identification and personal possessions, hold a service, and have a burial," he said. "It'll take the rest of the day. I want four men to rotate standing sentry." He dismounted and started down the slope, his troopers following. Fargo wanted to go his way but common decency vetoed the thought and he dismounted to add his back and hands to the grisly task.

When the bitter work was finished, night hung poised to descend, and Fargo rode back with the squad. The wounded men were hurried to Doc Schroder. Fargo unsaddled the Ovaro as the moon rose high. He had long missed the meal hour but when he entered the inn he saw Amanda beside the table and a buffalo sandwich waiting for him along with a mug of beer. "Thank you," he said as he sat down at the table. "You heard?" Amanda nodded and left him alone to eat, but not before her round, grave eyes had spoken to him and he nodded. When he finished, he stepped outside to see Doc Schroder leaning against the barracks wall, pipe in hand. "Sorry, no assistant," Fargo said.

"Rotten, all of it. I'm beginning to believe you were right from the very beginning," the army physician said.

"Cogswell tell you what he plans next?" Fargo queried.

"He's still convinced he can wipe out Red Bull. He still plans to bring him into open combat," the doctor said. "He'll give his men a day to rest while he prepares for another patrol."

"A stubborn, stupid man, caught up in his own plans for himself," Fargo said.

"Maybe he could win if he can get the damn Indians into a pitched battle," Schroder said.

"He wants Red Bull to fight on his terms. Red Bull will fight on his own terms," Fargo said.

"Kray's still in with Cogswell, telling him how right he is," the doctor said.

Fargo digested the information. "Either he's as stupid as the captain or a lot smarter," Fargo said. "Maybe if I can find out the answer to that I can still do something to stop this mass suicide."

"Good luck," the doctor said, and Fargo went into the inn and down the dim corridor. Amanda opened at his first knock and came to rest her head against his chest for a moment before stepping back. She turned quickly and the thin cotton nightdress swung against her to outline her lovely curves. She folded herself on the mattress and stared up at him, a hint of reproach in her eyes.

"Tomorrow," he said, reading her thoughts. "I won't let anything stop me tomorrow." Her eyes softened, but he refused to hold out hope, not to her, not to himself. Arlene had suddenly become a kind of last chance. Maybe whatever had made her run would make Burton Cogswell listen. It wasn't much of a last chance, he realized, but it was the only one left.

He started to take his shirt off. "I'm tired and I'll be gone early," he said. Amanda nodded but she didn't turn the lamp out until he had shed the last of his clothes. When he lay down, her head came to rest against his shoulder again. He raised his arm, started to draw her closer and felt her stiffen at once. He lowered his arm and she relaxed in moments. He felt her arm come across his chest and the side of her thigh touch his leg. He looked down at her. She lay with her eyes closed, her lovely face in complete repose. She was a model of innocent trust wrapped in sensuality, not unlike a picture in the wrong frame.

But she was certainly putting his self-discipline to the test. He closed his eyes, welcoming weariness, and slept heavily until dawn. He woke, slid from under her, and had finished dressing when she opened her eyes. She sat up as he slipped from the room. She'd understand, he knew. Outside, the barracks were still asleep and silent as he saddled the Ovaro and walked the horse from the area before climbing into the saddle. He didn't want questions from anyone, especially Cogswell. He rode hard, taking advantage of the early morning coolness before the sun began to bake the land.

As he rode, the sight of the twenty-five slain troopers returned to his mind. They marked the character of Red Bull. He was plainly very much a Northern Cheyenne chief, raised and trained to strike back with utter ruthlessness. Burton Cogswell was triggering the full-scale conflict but he brought only overweaning, callous ambition to the contest. That was no match for fierce pride and fiercer hate. Cogswell's brutality came from cold calculation. Red Bull's from a way of life. Again, there was no match. Fargo put away further thoughts as he reached the hilly plain and the stand of cottonwoods where he had left the Cheyenne girl. Red Flower, she had called herself, and he let the name stay on his tongue as he moved into the cottonwoods where she had disappeared from his sight.

He guessed she had gone in a fairly straight line and his guess was right as, a few hundred yards on, he picked up the set of lone footprints, smooth imprints made by moccasined feet. She had gone through the cottonwoods and out the other side, half running at first. The footprints had dug deeper into the soil, then slowed to a walk when she left the trees. She had crossed a rolling flatland filled with gopher holes and scurrying paw prints, and had climbed a hill dotted with serviceberry, and he followed. When he reached the top he found a flat table of land with a heavy overgrowth of red ash and he spotted her tracks where they had moved through a field of bittersweet nightshade whose brilliant red berries were a slash of color across the land.

He kept the pinto at a walk as he tracked the prints and pulled to a halt as his nostrils suddenly picked up the odor of fish oil blown on a soft breeze. He swung from the Ovaro, who followed on his heels as he moved forward. The fish oil mingled with another odor, and he sniffed the air. Bear grease, he decided. He could hear sounds, now, the murmur of voices. He crept forward more slowly. The murmur grew louder, the voices became distinct, and he halted, dropped the Ovaro's reins over a low branch, and went forward alone. He followed the sound now, peering through the trees as he moved on silent cat steps. Suddenly the camp came into view directly in front of him. He moved still closer before he halted and dropped to one knee.

He was not more than fifty yards from the camp now, and he saw at least eight tipis and a longhouse at one end. This was no hunting camp, but a full base encampment, and he saw some forty Indian ponies along the other side of the camp. His eyes moved across the scene, took in plenty of near-naked young braves, more than enough squaws, not all old women here but many young, some bare-breasted, others wearing their deerskin garments. A large tipi near the center of the camp caught his eye. Painted symbols circled the tan canvas. All the tipis used the three-pole, wide-base construction favored by the Cheyenne.

He let his gaze move across the camp again, saw the long, narrow cooking pits along one side, and searched among the young women for Red Flower. He felt his skin quiver as the two arrows thudded into the ground, one on each side of him. "Damn," he murmured as he forced himself not to try and leap away. There were other arrows aimed at his back, he knew, and he slowly stood up to see the one Indian come up behind him while the second one dropped down from a tree. "Damn," he swore again aloud. His own fault. He had been too intent on finding the camp, too concerned with peering at it. He hadn't been careful enough to look for sentries.

He hadn't expected any. Always a mistake not to expect sentries. Mistakes he knew better than to make and he had made them. The two Cheyenne came alongside him and the Colt was yanked from its holster. They gestured for him to walk and kept their drawn bows pointed at him. He started toward the camp, and they fell in behind him until he walked into the cleared land of the Cheyenne camp and heard the murmur of voices die to a hush. Eyes stared at him, only surprise in some but instant anger in others. The one sentry pointed to the tall tipi. He walked toward it, halting as the flap opened, and the figure emerged. He faced a man almost as tall as he, broad-shouldered, with a prominent nose and piercing black eyes in a commanding face framed with thick, heavily greased black hair. Bare-chested, with a well-muscled torso, the Indian wore deerskin leggings and a beaded choker around his neck with a shell disc at the center. A long, golden-eagle feather rose from the back of his black hair.

"Red Bull. Chief of the Northern Cheyenne," Fargo said in his best Algonquian. The Indian's broad face remained impassive and his eyes bored into Fargo as the two sentries spoke to him.

"You come to spy on Red Bull for the bluecoats," the Cheyenne chief said.

"No," Fargo answered and turned as he heard the voice call out. He saw the slender figure in the deer-skin dress stepping forward, her face as handsome as he remembered, the delicate, straight nose giving her an almost patrician cast. "Red Flower," he said. The Indian girl's black-brown eyes met his for a brief glance and then returned to the Cheyenne chief.

"He is the one," Fargo heard her say and this time Fargo saw surprise touch the man's impassive face. Red Flower spoke again to him, quick sentences of which Fargo only caught a few words. She had just finished when an old squaw stepped forward and spoke to Red Bull.

"He is the one who came to the camp to warn us of the bluecoat attack," Fargo heard her say and Red Bull turned to him, his black eyes narrowed in thought.

"Red Flower is my sister," the Cheyenne said. "You save her life. You save the lives of the old ones in the camp. Yet you help the bluecoats at our ambush." The Indian used sign language to help Fargo understand his words. "What kind of man are you?" the question came.

"I want to stop the killing," Fargo said, and Red Bull gave a derisive snort. Fargo's mind raced as he searched for a way to reach the chief who, with that immediate response, had told him it would be impossible to stop the killing. He drew on an analogy the Indian would understand and used sign language to supplement what Algonquian he could muster. "The small fires will go on. I want to stop the big fire. I want to stop the fire that will destroy the forest," he said.

He waited, saw Red Bull turn his answer over. "You save Red Flower. You save my people at the camp. You save the bluecoats at our ambush. No man can be a friend to everyone," the Cheyenne said. Fargo cursed silently at the truth of simple wisdoms. "Why did you come here?" Red Bull asked.

Fargo drew the tintype from his pocket and showed it to the chief and saw Red Flower lean forward to look. "I come to find this woman," Fargo said. "The soldier chief says you have taken her," he added and used the sign for capture.

Red Bull's eyes didn't flicker as he handed the tintype back. "We did not capture her," he said and duplicated the sign for capture Fargo had used. "She is not here."

"Pony marks were found where she was taken," Fargo said.

Red Bull shrugged. "The Cheyenne are not alone in this land," he said. "You have saved Red Flower. The Cheyenne pay back their enemies. The Cheyenne pay back their friends. You may stay the night and search the camp for this woman."

Fargo realized the magnitude of the concession. It was also plain that it wouldn't have been offered if Arlene were in the camp, and he decided to return the slightly empty magnanimity. "I take Red Bull's word," he said.

The Cheyenne nodded. "Then you will stay the night as our guest," he said. "When day comes, you can go alive."

Fargo half bowed. The message was clear. He was being given his life in return for having befriended Red Flower and the old ones at the hunting camp. Red Bull turned abruptly and strode into the tipi. The

91

others drifted away and Fargo found himself with Red Flower as the night descended. "Come," she said, and he followed her to the longhouse where she entered and lighted a wick atop a stone filled with tallow. The flickering light afforded a shadowy illumination in the longhouse, but Fargo saw the bearskin rugs on the floor. "I did not expect to see you again, man who makes trails," Red Flower said.

"Fargo," he smiled. "And I did not expect to find you the sister of the great Cheyenne chief."

She gave a little shrug. "I do not always agree with his ways but he is the chief and he is made of stone," the young woman said. "You will be brought food," she told him as she turned and stepped from the longhouse without a glance back. Fargo lowered himself to the bearskin rugs and cursed softly. He was alive, despite the stupid mistakes he had made, and he was grateful for that. But he felt a sense of futility. The visit had been a waste of time. Arlene was not here and the Cheyenne chief had been adamant in insisting they hadn't captured her. Perhaps it had been a passing band of Arapaho, Fargo pondered. He hadn't considered that, but perhaps it was time to do so. If so, any chance of finding Arlene was gone.

He was wondering why Desmond Kray had been so insistent it had to have been Red Bull when the two squaws entered the longhouse carrying wooden bowls of food. They set the bowls down in front of him, along with a stone cup of liquid, backed away, and left without a word. He realized he was hungry as he began to eat and found the food tasty enough, recognizing prairie turnip, berries, squash, and a little antelope. The liquid was sweet and tasted of apple juice. He lay back when he finished. The longhouse held the warmth of the day in it. He took off his shirt and gunbelt when the figure came in and he saw Red Flower, clothed only in a calfskin skirt.

He felt his lips go dry for a moment as he took in the beauty of her, skin coppery and smooth in the flickering light, her breasts not large but beautifully rounded and perfectly placed on her slender torso, nipples a deep pinkish brown on a lighter-toned areola. She sank down on both knees in front of him and he saw a tiny smile edge her lips as she watched his eyes linger on her breasts. "Red Flower pleases you?" she murmured.

"Red Flower is beautiful," he said.

"The one you seek, she is your woman?" Red Flower asked.

"No, she is not my woman," Fargo answered.

"Why do you seek her?"

"I want to bring her back and show the chief of the bluecoats that she is safe. That may stop the big killing," Fargo said. She fell silent and her eyes stared down at the bearskin rugs and Fargo frowned as he sensed something unsaid. "You do not want the big killing do you?" he asked, deciding to gamble.

"No, I do not want it. It frightens me," she said. "But it is not for me to say."

"Did Red Bull speak the truth about the girl?" Fargo pressed.

"Yes," Red Flower said and lifted her eyes to meet his. "But I did not come to talk of that," she said, and with a sudden motion she pulled at the side of the calfskin skirt and it fell away. She knelt beautifully naked in front of him and he took in a smallish figure, almost petite, but a flat belly, just the hint of nap atop the small protruberance of her pubic mound. Her thighs were full for the rest of her, yet smoothly muscled and shining with copper-hued loveliness. "Red

93

Bull has let you live to repay you for saving my life. But it is not his to repay you. It is mine."

Fargo reached a hand out, touched her shoulder. "Words will be enough," he said. "Thank you is not the same as wanting." She blinked at him and he saw she hadn't fully understood. He used sign language with words as he tried again. "To make love is not for honor," he said. "It is for wanting."

She thought for a moment and a slow smile came to her lips. She leaned forward and her arms slid around his neck. Her nose nuzzled against his, and her lips moved with tiny, nibbling motions across his face. "Not for honor," she murmured as she nuzzled him and her breasts came to press into his chest, the small, flat pink-brown nipples a delicately provocative touch. He let her arms stay around his neck and slid the trousers from his legs as Red Flower rubbed her breasts slowly up and down against his chest. He half turned with her, cupped one hand around one of the round mounds, let his thumb pass slowly back and forth over the small nipple, and felt it grow under his touch, rising, its own tiny erection.

He brought his mouth down to the perfectly shaped, small mound, drew the smooth copper-hued flesh up against his tongue. The Indian girl moaned, a soft, sighing sound, breathy yet fevered, and the soft moans continued as his tongue caressed her nipple and his lips pulled gently on her breast. "Aaaaah . . . aaaaaaa-aaaah . . ." she moaned. The moan became a singsong sound that rose and fell almost in rhythm with the movement of her hips as his hand traced a path downward along the smooth copper skin to rest on the nearly hairless pubic mound. He caressed and pressed as his mouth clung to her breast and Red Flower's thighs fell open, came together, and fell open once again. He felt her hands pressing into his buttocks, pulling at him, and he came atop her. Her moan rose suddenly, growing sharper but continuing its singsong undulation. He brought his pulsating warmth to her and felt the smoothness of her, and suddenly her legs were clasped around his waist and her hips thrust upward and upward again.

He slid forward into the dark warmth and felt her almost smooth pubic mound rise up to slap against his groin. He slid forward again, drew back, came forward, exulted in the smoothness of her passage and felt her hands, little fists now, pounding against his ribs and her moaning now in complete rhythm with every thrust of her hips. He stayed with her, matching her every upward thrust and felt her movements quicken and grow stronger and sharper. Suddenly the long soft moaning broke off and instead her lips opened up in short, tiny, almost barklike sounds. Her copper-hued thighs opened and slammed against him and her body clung to his. Her hands dug into his back and her knees drew up and she became rigid, suspended against him. The short, staccato sounds continued to come from her until suddenly they ended in an abrupt growling, a cry of protest and pleasure and her body fell away from his.

She lay on her back on the bearskin rug, the smallish, perfectly rounded breasts lifting and falling as she gasped in deep breaths of air. He rested beside her and enjoyed the strong, lithe beauty of her as she grew calm, her black-brown eyes focused on him. Her arms reached up, hands clasping around his neck, and she drew him down to press his face into her breasts. She held him there with a sigh of contentment and it wasn't long before he heard the steady sound of her sleep. He let his eyes close. Sleep came to him as he lay against the silk-soft pillows, as comforting a bed as any man could want.

He slept well and woke when he felt her stir. He pulled his eyes open and saw her slip from him, half roll, and pull the calfskin skirt to herself. She had it wrapped around her waist in seconds and she rose, came to him, and held his face into her breasts once again. "Not for honor," she murmured, the tiny smile on her lips again, and as she stepped lightly through the doorway he saw the first gray light of dawn outside.

He lay back, blew out the tallow stone, let himself enjoy another few hours of sleep, and woke when the sun found a way to filter into the longhouse. He rose, climbed into trousers, and stepped outside to see the camp waking. A small stream ran along the back edge near the ponies and he stepped to it and washed, drawing only glances of passing interest as he did. He knelt beside the stream and let the sun half dry him before he donned his clothes again and made his way across the camp. He saw the flap of the large tipi open. Red Bull emerged, the shell-disc choker around his neck but now with a wide, beaded tie hanging down from it. Fargo halted before the Cheyenne chief's impassive face.

"You will go, now," the Indian said. "Tell your bluecoats that we did not capture the woman."

"I will," Fargo said. He saw Red Flower walk toward him, the deerskin dress over her lovely body and in her eyes a tiny, satisfied glint, unsaid words. He smiled back. "Maybe we meet another day, a better day," he said to her. She let her eyes answer.

"Go," Red Bull intoned, his voice deepening. Fargo turned and saw four braves waiting on their ponies for him, each carrying arrows and bow and a tomahawk in the waistband of his breechclout. One held the Ovaro, he saw with a half-smile, less of surprise than grudging admiration. They had searched the woods to make certain he had no company with him and found the horse. He swung onto the Ovaro and walked the horse from the camp as a brave came along each side of him and two rode at his back.

He turned in the saddle to glance back and offer a friendly wave. Others had gathered to watch him ride away and his glance moved across a line of squaws and suddenly something slammed into his gut. No physical blow but it might just as well have been, as he felt the breath sucked from him in shocked surprise. One of the squaws wore a purple sash around her waist.

6

He turned away and rode slowly as he fought through the whirl of thoughts that raced through his mind like a stampede of longhorns. The Cheyenne chief had lied to him. Arlene was in their hands. Red Bull had flatly lied. Surprised as he was, Fargo could accept that. But Red Flower had lied, also. It seemed a betrayal, somehow. She had given herself to him, wildly and wholly, and had lied to him. It was not usual Indian behavior. It violated their intrinsic code of honor. But she had done it. She had laid and lied.

Why, he asked himself again. Because his direct question had backed her into a corner? Because she couldn't bring herself to say her brother had lied to him? Because she had to go along with his deceit? The reasons were all possible, but the end result was the same. They had taken Arlene. He broke off his thoughts as the four braves came to a halt. One drew the Colt from under his breechclout and gave it to him and Fargo nodded thanks as he holstered the gun. The four stayed in place, waited, and watched as he moved the Ovaro forward through the forest, and he finally heard them leave when he was beyond their sight.

The urge to turn around and go back pulled at him but he flung it aside. That would be suicide, he realized. Red Bull would have sentries surrounding the camp. He'd take no chances now. Perhaps he'd anticipate the intruder trying to return. Not now, Fargo muttered silently, and put the Ovaro into a trot as thoughts flooded over him again. Two facts emerged clearly. Arlene wasn't at the Cheyenne camp. Red Bull would never have offered to let him search if she had been there. But she had been. They had taken her. The squaw's purple sash was damming proof. Desmond Kray had been right after all. Luck or something else? Answers still danced out of reach and death still waited in the wings.

He rode on through the morning and into the afternoon with the sense of futility clinging to him. He had nothing to make the captain pull back, nothing to provide answers to anything. His lips drew back in distaste as he realized that the only way to find answers could be to pay another visit to the Cheyenne camp. It would be returning to almost certain death, he knew. Red Bull had paid his debt of honor. There would be no other concessions. He'd try Amanda again, first, he decided. Maybe there was something she hadn't thought to tell him, some little thing that might not be so little.

The day was nearing dusk when he arrived back at Kray's Corners, wondering if he could find a way to free Amanda from her bond of silence. Maybe if he could get her to talk he might be able to pull more from her. If there was a way. If, he grunted with frustration.

Desmond Kray sauntered over to him when he dismounted. "I thought maybe you'd left without saying good-bye," Kray remarked.

"Wouldn't think of it," Fargo said. "Anything been happening?"

"The captain came onto four squaws picking berries with two old men looking after them this morning," Kray said. "There are six less of the damn savages now." He grinned, pleased with the thought. "Soon it'll be Red Bull coming out. That's all the captain wants."

Fargo felt his stomach knot. The wheels continued to turn toward a bloodbath. "The last time Red Bull came out the captain lost twenty-five new reinforcements," he reminded Kray, bitterness in his voice.

Kray shrugged. "The captain's ready for him this time," he said and strode away. Fargo turned as dusk slid into night. He saw Doc Schroder nearby.

"You get the feeling you're on a sinking ship?" Fargo asked the doctor. "If you don't, you should."

"I keep wishing you aren't right and keep feeling you are," the army physician said.

"Let me lean on your professional opinion again, Doc," Fargo said. "What could get Amanda to talk again, if she ever could?"

"Opinion is the right word. We don't know enough about the human mind to answer that. If she's suffering from deep shock, an emotional shutdown, it could take years to come out of it, if she ever did. It depends on what's happened inside her. The mind works in funny ways. I've heard that sometimes survivors feel guilty about surviving. Going into deep emotional shock is a kind of self-punishment. Other times there's no guilt, just such a searing experience they can't handle the effects, and a part of them withdraws from the world."

"Sounds like you're saying there's nothing that can be done."

"No, I'm saying it's damn hard to find a way to do anything, but I know of cases where shock has made people snap back."

"Shock?" Fargo frowned.

"Such as coming face-to-face with the same experience that made them snap. Or some other experience that can shock them out of it. Whatever it is, the key is intenseness. They have to be touched by something intense enough to reach down inside them and unlock the inner feelings they've locked away, something intense enough to make them come fully alive again."

"Thanks," Fargo said. "Not that you've given me much encouragement."

"Sorry," Schroder said. Fargo went into the inn and saw Amanda waiting in the dimness. She beckoned to him and fled to her room as he followed. Inside, she clung to him, arms clutching him around the waist, her body trembling.

"Easy," he said, stroking the light brown hair with one hand, and finally she stepped back, the round brown orbs grave. She made her sign for being afraid and then pointed at him. "You were afraid for me," he said and she nodded. "Thank you," he said, realizing that it sounded both inappropriate and very appropriate. "The Cheyenne have Arlene. Or they took her. I learned that much but I didn't find her."

Amanda sank down on the mattress and motioned for him to sit beside her. "I was inside their camp. She wasn't there," he said. "But she was there. One of the squaws wore her sash." He paused. "I think she's still alive," he said and realized he could offer nothing to justify the feeling. Yet it was real. There were shadows inside shadows hiding in more than one place, he was convinced. He lay back on the mattress and realized he was tired, perhaps as much inside as outside. "I need you to think more, Amanda, any little thing you can remember," he said.

Amanda pounded her fist on her forehead, rocked back and forth, and then turned her palms up helplessly. "You have been thinking," Fargo said. "And you can't come up with anything." She nodded and dropped her hands into her lap. He was growing quite adept at reading her gestures, he told himself approvingly. It was really the only positive thing he could point to. "Time to sleep," he said and began to undress. Once again Amanda didn't turn the lamp out until he had finished, and when he lay down she came against him, her head all the way against his shoulder this time and her thigh touching his. He raised his arm and cradled her into the hollow of his shoulder. She stayed without protest, one arm draping itself across his chest again.

He looked down at her face. Her eyes were closed already, her other hand against her cheek little-girl-like. But the curve of one breast over the neckline of the nightdress was anything but little-girl-like. What would happen to her when he went on his way, he wondered. The answer struck into him as though it were a slap. Would he be going his way? Would any of them? He could just ride out, he knew, and snorted inwardly. It had been a mocking thought that had grown more so with every passing day. Stupidity, stubbornness, conscience, sometimes it was hard to tell them apart. He'd see it through until there was nothing left to see through.

He closed his eyes and let sleep sweep away all else.

7

Amanda was up first with the new sun, and she took her things outside to wash and dress. He was finished when she returned in the shapeless brown dress. "I'll be back tonight," he told her, her eyes showed she understood. He went outside where he drank a mug of coffee and saw Kray leaning against the door of the trading post, watching him with a curiosity in his darting eyes. Fargo turned and walked to the lean-to. He never blamed a man for wondering, but Kray made wondering into obscene prying.

Fargo saddled up and rode alongside the barracks as Cogswell halted at the head of his men, everyone saddled and ready to ride. "Heard you were back," the captain said. "I'm afraid I have things going according to plan."

"Those twenty-five reinforcements were according to plan?" Fargo said with mock surprise and enjoyed seeing Cogswell's face stiffen.

"A momentary setback. It happens in the finest of campaigns," the captain said.

"That makes me feel a lot better," Fargo said and sent the Ovaro into a fast trot. He wanted to get away alone, ride the hills, and pull his thoughts together. He sent the Ovaro up a steep slope, then another, and rode west along the highland. As the sun grew warmer he slowed to a walk and picked his way along rocky passages thick with wiry brush until he came to a high plains. He tried to think of a way to reach Cogswell and again realized he hadn't any. The man was fired by ruthless ambition but also by self-delusion. He seemed suffused with a smug self-confidence that even his lack of experience didn't justify. Another visit to the Cheyenne main camp seemed the only remaining hope. But now Fargo was unsure if even returning with Arlene would lessen the captain's determination to engage the Cheyenne.

Grimness riding with him, Fargo turned south and saw three small settlements some thousand yards apart from each other nestled in a green patch of land. He turned the Ovaro toward the nearest one. As he neared it he saw a pen of some twenty pigs along one side of a modest cabin. There was a field of squash and turnips stretched out to the rear. A man, a young boy, and a woman came out of the house as he rode to a halt and he glimpsed two younger children at a window peering out. All carried rifles. He saw relief in their faces as they stopped before him. "You alone, mister?" the man asked, and Fargo nodded.

"Just riding through," Fargo said.

"Watch yourself. Saw a damn big band of Cheyenne less than an hour ago," the man said.

"How many?" Fargo asked.

"Too many. They were a good way off, along Bluecap Ridge," the man said and pointed to a distant ridge lined with blue spruce.

"You never know what a big party like that means. Maybe you and the other folks around here ought to pick up and go camp out at the army barracks at Kray's Corners for a spell," Fargo suggested.

"Nobody likes to leave their home. An empty house is an invitation to getting burned down," the man said.

"Nobody likes to leave their scalp, either," Fargo said. "Think about it." He rode off with a wave and pointed the pinto for the ridge, climbed a long slope to reach it, and quickly found the pony tracks along the top of the ridge line. He reined to a halt as the furrow dug into his brow. He had expected tracks from the south, Red Bull taking a full war party out. But these hoofprints came from the west. They moved southward but from the west. Of course the Cheyenne chief could have made a circle, but Fargo turned the Ovaro and began to trace the prints back the way they had come.

Too many for a hunting party, he noted. Thirty or more ponies, he guessed. They rode Indian file along the ridge and he followed the prints westward where they dipped down onto lowland. No circling, he noted as the prints bunched up where they had ridden close together. The track turned, led northwest, but there was no circle up from the south, and Fargo pulled to a halt. These were not Red Bull's braves, he told himself and felt his stomach tighten. He wheeled the horse around and retracted the way he'd come, back onto the ridge and on, following the tracks where they moved down onto lower land at the other end of the ridge. He stopped to pick up a small deerskin pouch and read the beadwork on it. Cheyenne, he thought as he moved on and saw the tracks going south, on a direct line to Red Bull's camp.

He drew to a halt. The tightness inside him had grown tighter. Cheyenne, but not Red Bull's own braves. These had come from the northwest. Red Bull had called on another band of Cheyenne for reinforcements. He was preparing to mount a major attack. He had called in enough warriors to paint the territory red with blood. Fargo turned again and put the pinto into a fast canter as he rode back toward Kray's Corners. He had something to make Cogswell listen, now, if it wasn't too late.

He rode hard, and the day neared its end when he reached the barracks. He saw the men brushing down their mounts and knew Cogswell had returned. He strode to the captain's quarters, found the door open, and marched in.

Cogswell looked up from behind his desk, a regional chart spread out before him. "Choosing the best place to finish the job," the captain said.

"You've got to pull back," Fargo said.

"You're becoming amusing," Cogswell returned. "He's afraid. He'll come out to do battle. He has to but he's afraid. I've wiped out two groups of his people in the last two days and he hasn't struck back once. He's afraid."

"He's gotten reinforcements. A Cheyenne band from the north. They'll outnumber you two to one, maybe more," Fargo said.

"Is that so?" Cogswell said and sat back. "Even better. My victory will be even more complete." Fargo stared incredulously at the smug smile that slid across the captain's face.

"I don't believe what I'm hearing," Fargo said.

"Believe it. I told you I'm prepared to wipe out Red Bull and I am," Cogswell said as he rose and strode to the door. "Come along, Fargo," he barked, and Fargo followed him outside where he strode to the last structure at the end of the stables. He pushed the door open and lit a kerosene lamp hanging on the wall. Fargo saw a storage shed with boxes and crates strewn about. Cogswell pulled the lid up on one crate and Fargo peered inside. Six sticks of dynamite lay in a neat row inside the crate. "They're going to get a lot more than rifle fire," Cogswell said. "This will more than make up for their extra warriors." Fargo met the captain's gaze and saw the triumph in Cogswell's face. "You see, Fargo, I'm not the fool you keep insisting I am."

"Fool. Conceited ass. Madman. Babe in the woods. It all comes out the same. Your lousy six sticks of dynamite won't win for you. You'll surprise them, kill a handful. But only once. They'll make adjustments real fast," Fargo said.

"You'll see, Fargo. You'll see," Cogswell said as he closed the lid on the box.

"That's what I'm afraid of," Fargo muttered and strode outside. He hurried into the inn and down the corridor to Amanda's room, where she held herself against him in a silence that was not really silent at all. He held her gently, letting her cling until she finally stepped back. He took her hand and folded himself onto the mattress with her. "I'm going back. I have to try to find her. Bringing her back might be the only thing that'll slow Cogswell down. If it's not already too late," Fargo said with a grimness he knew was all too justified. "I'll go in the morning so's I reach the Cheyenne after dark." Amanda took his hand and squeezed it between both of hers. "I'll be careful," he said. "Now it's time to get some sleep."

Amanda nodded and turned out the lamp at once. He heard her shedding clothes and pulling the night-dress on before his eyes could adjust to the dim light of the moon. She was in the nightdress, sitting on the mattress, when he undressed and lay down. She leaned her head on his shoulder at once. He felt the softness of her thigh against his leg as she settled down against him, once again embracing sensuality and in-nocence. But this night, instead of her arm draping across his chest, her hand came up to rest gently against his face, words of touch, silence that spoke its own language. He closed his eyes, cradling her head against him, and slept.

He had no idea how long he'd slept when he came awake, sitting bolt upright as the shot shattered sleep. Amanda rolled to one side and brought herself up on her haunches. The room was still cloaked in darkness. Another shot rang out and then shouts. He sprang from the mattress, yanked on trousers and gunbelt, and saw Amanda pulling the brown garment on over the nightdress. "Stay here," he flung at her as he raced from the room, the Colt in his hand. As he ran down the corridor and through the front room of the inn, he saw a flickering glow from outside, and when he reached into the darkness he saw a corner of the nearest barracks building on fire. Two more fire arrows hurtled through the night to imbed themselves into the side of the next building and he saw the captain's two sentries lying on the ground, both riddled with arrows.

Troopers were pouring out of the barracks now, most only half dressed but all with their carbines in hand. They milled around, uncertain of what to do. Fargo ran forward in a low crouch as three more flaming arrows hurled from the blackness to land on the roof of the nearest barracks. The dry wood came on fire at once and he saw the captain, clad in trousers and boots, racing toward his men as he shouted commands. "Ten men on the fires. Buckets and the water from the horse troughs," he ordered. "The rest of you prepare to counterattack but stay low."

The fires were quickly gathering strength, sending an orange glow skyward and lighting the ground nearby. "You go out there and you'll lose half your men," Fargo said. "That's just what they want. You'll make perfect targets against the firelight." Cogswell halted and peered at him for a moment. "Put most of your men on dousing the fires," Fargo said.

Cogswell spun and barked new orders to his men

and Fargo dropped to one knee at a corner of the barracks. A sudden volley of rifle fire made him dive for cover. He saw some of the troopers flatten themselves on the ground. Cogswell had his men return fire from a prone position but they were shooting blindly into the darkness. Fargo's eyes caught a glimpse of shadowy figures near the trading post and saw three more fire arrows slam into the front of the building. He circled back around the rear of the inn and had made his way toward the small space between the two structures when he glimpsed the figures running toward him. He dropped to the ground as they saw him and fired, rifle fire, and he saw three dive through a side window into the inn while the fourth one continued to pin him down with gunfire.

Fargo swore as he rolled behind the corner of the inn, pushed to his feet, and ran back beneath the lean-to and the window of his room. He pushed the window open, swung into the room, and raced across it and out into the hallway. He heard the sound of the guttural shouts from the front room as he ran, and he came to a halt as he saw two Cheyenne dragging Amanda across the floor. He brought the Colt up and fired as he raced forward. Both Cheyenne flew backward as the heavy slugs slammed into them. Amanda flattened herself against the floor. Fargo whirled in time to see another form charging at him, tomahawk raised. Fargo tried to bring the Colt up but the man was too close and he had to twist away to avoid a slashing blow of the axe. He half fell, half spun to one side, brought the gun around, fired, and saw the shot graze the Indian's ribs as the man dived at him again.

Fargo dropped low, and the Indian slammed into him, diving over his back. Fargo straightened and sent the figure somersaulting. He whirled, as the Cheyenne hit the floor, raised the Colt, and fired; the Indian's chest exploded in a shower of red. Fargo started to straighten up when he caught the sound from behind him and remembered there had been four Indians in the alleyway. He dropped, certain there wasn't time to turn, but he felt the side of the tomahawk scrape along his temple. Colored lights exploded in front of him as he fell and the Colt flew from his grip when he hit the floor. He rolled, his temple throbbing and the lights still flashing, but he heard the thud of footsteps and he flung himself sideways again. The sound only inches from his ear was unmistakable, followed by the crash of the tomahawk blade into the floorboards.

Fargo shook his head and the colored lights disappeared, to be replaced by the figure of the Cheyenne yanking the blade of his tomahawk out of the floor. It took the man only seconds, but seconds were enough for Fargo to swing to his feet and face the Indian in a half-crouch. He let his attacker move at him, the Cheyenne holding the short-handled axe high, ready to strike with it. Fargo shifted right, then left, then right again, and with an impatient roar the Cheyenne charged. Fargo held in place, counted off split seconds, and watched the blade come down at him. He shifted again, smashing his forearm against his attacker's wrist with just enough force to deflect the blow as he brought his right up in a hard smash into the man's abdomen. The Indian grunted as he doubled over, and Fargo smashed his shoulder into the man's lowered face. The Cheyenne went backward, staggered, and took Fargo's looping left on the point of the jaw. He fell and the tomahawk dropped from his hand.

The weapon was closer than the Colt. Fargo bent down to scoop it up, but the Indian kicked out, a wavering blow that grazed Fargo's leg. Fargo's hand closed around the tomahawk and he struck out with it in a backhanded whirl as the Cheyenne started to push to his feet. The axe crashed into the side of his head and he went down, this time to stay down. Fargo ran to where Amanda still lay facedown on the floor, scooping up the Colt as he did. He lifted her up and looked into her face. There were no tears, only the terror in her round eyes. "Go back to your room. Stay there," he said as he led her down the corridor. "I'll come back." Amanda went soundlessly with him and he saw her fall onto the mattress before he pulled the door shut.

He ran back through the front room, leaped over the slain forms, and raced outside where the troopers were still laying down a rifle fire barrage, most firing from their prone positions on the ground. But the fires had been put out and the air smelled of charred wood and smoke. Fargo dropped to one knee beside Cogswell, who crouched at a corner of the barracks. There were no more fire arrows hurtling from the darkness and no answering rifle fire. "They're gone," he said. "Your men are just wasting ammunition."

"Cease fire," Cogswell shouted, and the soldiers stopped shooting. The captain rose up and turned to Fargo. "They caught us by surprise but they didn't mount a real attack. Typical Indian tactics. They don't understand the principles of warfare."

"It was a raid. They didn't plan to attack you inside your barrack walls," Fargo said. "They figured your men would come running out and they could cut down enough of them before disappearing. You don't understand the principles of raiding."

Cogswell returned an impatient snort as a young-faced soldier approached, close-cropped red hair over a freckled forehead. "Two dead, two men slightly injured fighting the fires, Captain," the man said.

"Put six men out on sentry duty, Lieutenant Wilson," Cogswell said. "Each man in sight of another."

"Yes, sir," the young officer said and hurried away.

"Better late than never," Fargo said and drew a glare from the captain.

"That Indian's days are numbered, Fargo," Cogswell said tightly and strode back to his quarters.

Fargo let a deep sigh escape him. A lot of people's days were numbered if Cogswell had his way. Amanda flew into his mind. "Good God, Amanda," he said out loud as something close to guilt flooded over him. He spun on his heel and raced toward the inn, reached the doorway just as Kray appeared. The man held a six-gun and there was fear in his darting eyes. "Where the hell have you been?" Fargo tossed at him as he halted.

"I was out there, shootin' at them," Kray said.

"I didn't see you," Fargo frowned.

"I was around the other side of the trading post," Kray said. It was possible, but the nervousness in the man's face marked his words as lies. Fargo hurried past and down the corridor to Amanda's room. He burst into the room, slamming the door shut after him. She was huddled on the mattress in the pale light of the moon, rolled almost into a little ball. As he dropped to his knees beside her she lifted her head, and then her arms were tightly around his neck and she was clinging to him with all her strength.

He let her cling, held her, then slowly stroked her back with one hand. "It's over. They've gone," he said soothingly. "It's over." Slowly her body relaxed but she continued to hold him and he continued to stroke her back. Finally her arms slid from around his neck and she lay back on the mattress, her hands on his shoulders, her wide, deep brown eyes staring hard at him. He felt the pressure of her hands as she pulled him down beside her and he stretched out with her. She turned away, half rolled across the mattress and turned the lamp on low. It made a soft yellow light, barely filling the room, yet enough to dispel the darkness. Amanda rolled back against him and leaned her head on his chest, and he could feel the warmth of her even through the two garments she wore.

She stayed motionless against him, her face resting on his chest as he held one arm around her. He was filled with relief. He'd been afraid the experience might have shattered her further but she seemed no worse for it. She had developed her own strength, perhaps partly because of her silence, he realized. As she lay back, her face against him, he found himself thinking about two things that pushed at him about the attack. It had been a raid, no full attack, yet a night raid was most unusual for the Cheyenne. Like most Indians, they didn't favor fighting at night, though such night raids did sometimes occur. Then why did a handful break into the inn? An attempt to break into the captain's quarters would have been more likely. To kill or capture the bluecoat chief would have been a real coup. But they hadn't gone around to the rear of the barracks. They'd come to the rear of the inn. It didn't fit right. But then, very little fit right in any of this.

His thoughts broke off as Amanda's head changed position and he felt a softness against his chest. A furrow slid across his brow as he realized the softness was the touch of her lips. She had her lips pressed against his chest and was slowly moving them upward, a nibbling motion along his smoothly muscled chest. Then her head lifted, and the dark, brown eyes peered into his own. Her face came toward his and then Amanda's lips were upon his with a soft pressure and sweet taste, and he returned the kiss, letting his mouth press hers. Her lips opened for him. He felt the tip of her tongue touch his own, and he paused, pulling back to search her face. He saw only intenseness. Then Amanda's mouth was on his again, pushing, urging, wanting, and suddenly she tore away, reached both arms up and back and whisked off the brown garment and the nightdress in one motion.

She flung both aside and knelt before him beautifully naked. He gasped at the loveliness of her. He took in her perfectly shaped breasts, milk-white with cups full and shaped so that the very delicate pink nipples thrust upward, their tips flat and virginal, each areola a matching delicate pink. Beneath her breasts a round, full rib cage gave her body substance as a slender waist curved out in modest hips and long thighs that were deliciously shaped. A slightly convex little belly rounded itself down to a very black, very dense triangle that invited by its very bushiness. Amanda came to him again, arms sliding around his neck, and he pulled her onto her back. His hand curled around one lovely white breast, feeling its smooth softness, and his fingers caressed the delicate pink, flat nipple which rose at his touch.

His glance went to Amanda. Her eyes were open wide, almost staring, her lips parted. As he caressed the pink tip her hands became little fists that she pounded into the mattress. A glow of pleasure suffused her face, giving it a pinkish color. As his lips found her breasts her arms lifted and came down hard against the mattress. He sucked, gently pulled, caressing each lovely breast with his mouth and tongue, and Amanda's hands came up to dig into his back. He let his own hand trace a slow, sensual path down her torso, circle the little indentation in her belly, and then move down to the bushy, black triangle. He slid his fingers through the denseness, found it surprisingly soft with none of the usual fibril touch to it. He pressed gently, felt the swell of her Venus mound, and let his fingers dip lower, sliding downward to the end of the dense triangle.

His hand pressed into the soft flesh of her tightly held thighs and felt the wetness of them. Then, as one fingertip touched the very edge of the portal, Amanda's thighs flew open, quivered for a moment and clapped together again. He pressed further and Amanda's thighs fell open again, firm and lovely wands that now waved open and closed and then open again and he felt her torso pushing upward. He touched deeper, across the now thoroughly moist clitoral smoothness, surrogate lips that begged for caresses. Amanda's hands were fists again, pounding into his ribs. He brought his throbbing warmth over her bushy triangle and let it rest there for a moment. Amanda's eyes were closed, her mouth open and drawing in gasped breaths, her face wreathed in ecstasy. He brought his bulbous throbbing gift to her, slid forward, felt the tightness surround him, and halted as he saw the flash of pain cross Amanda's face, but her eyes had opened and she stared at him. She nodded with quick shakes of her head and her hands pulled on him, urging him forward.

He slid deeper. The momentary pain in her face gave way to a smile. She nodded again and again, and he pressed fully into her and saw her mouth stay open, gasping in breath. He began to move slowly, back and forth through the sweet passage made smooth by its warm moistness, and Amanda's head tossed from side to side on the sheet, her eyes open, a wildness in their brown depths and her lips working soundlessly as she gasped in pleasure. He pressed again and again. Her pubic mound rose to meet his every thrust, her soundless ecstasy reached new heights of intensity, and she pulled his face down to her breasts.

He clasped one nipple in his lips, then the other, and she held him there. He felt her surging with him and felt his climax quickening, the body running away, pleasure refusing to be harnessed. Suddenly Amanda's legs came up and tightened around him. He was being constricted, inside and outside, and her quick, throbbing, spasmodic clasping surrounded him. He lifted his head and saw Amanda's neck arch backward even as her back arched. Her mouth open, wild staring in her eyes, her arms were pulling him to her again. Her legs drew up further and she clung to him as she quivered and heaved and then as she came she gave not a cry, not a scream, but a shriek, a wild, vaulting shriek, a bursting sound made of the ecstasy of release.

"Oh, God, oh God . . . aaaaiiiieeee . . . oh, miGod, oh, miGod," the words came and he wanted to laugh, or perhaps cry, as Amanda clung to him and gasped out more words, a running, tumbling stream of words. "Oh, God, oh wonderful . . . wonderful . . . miGod, again, again, more . . . oh, Jesus, more . . . more." The words trailed off, her voice ended in breathy gasps, and he drew back, still inside her as her thighs stayed clasped around her.

"In time . . . in time," he murmured and his hand caressed her face. "You talked, honey-face, you talked, you cried out," he said and she nodded and smiled at him. "No more silence," he said and she nodded again.

"No more," she whispered against him and her legs fell away and she gave a sigh of contented protest as he slid back to lay half over her.

"You made it happen, Fargo," Amanda said softly.

"You wanted it to happen," he said. "Somewhere, deep inside yourself, you wanted to talk again."

Amanda's lips took on a mischievous, Cheshire-cat smile. "I wanted this to happen," she said. "From the first day you came here. I didn't know it would be like this. I didn't know it would make everything happen."

Fargo smiled as he thought about Doc Schroder's words. Intenseness, the doctor had said, something intense enough to reach deep down inside and unlock inner feelings. His prognosis had been right but he hadn't considered this methodology. Amanda turned, left him for a moment, and put the lamp off as the morning sun began to creep into the room. She rolled back to him, a picture of lovely, lithe grace, the perfectly shaped breasts swinging in unison, their delicate pink tips coming to rest against his chest, softly tickling. But he saw her deep brown eyes grow grave.

"I can say it, now. I'm afraid, Fargo. I don't want you to go after Arlene and not come back," she said, and he frowned at the smile that came to her face with a flash of suddenness. "It feels so good to talk again," she said. "So wonderful."

He smiled and understood, as much as it was possible for anyone to understand. "I have to go after Arlene. She's the last chance to maybe stop the killing that'll sure as hell happen," he said, and he rose and went to the washbasin. Amanda waited, watched, and handed him a towel when he finished. She washed as he dressed, and he enjoyed the beautiful grace of her every motion. When she finished she went to the clothes on the wall peg and brought out a yellow dress that she slipped on to stand before him, lovely as a buttercup. It was a statement of its own, he realized, a coming out, a reemergence. No more shapeless brown garments.

She left the room with him and he saw a lift to her

chin, her eyes bright, a new firmness in her step. She stepped outside with him where he saw Doc Schroder having his morning pipe, his face serious. The doctor turned to him as Fargo approached, Amanda alongside. "You look preoccupied this morning, Doc," Fargo commented.

"The captain's preparing to move out in force, probably tomorrow," Doc Schroder said. "He's taking every man we have, including me. I'm to be there to treat field casualties on the spot."

Fargo made a quick count in his head, eliminating the men that had already been lost. "That gives him some fifty-four men," he said.

"He expects his dynamite will count for the twenty-five troopers that never arrived," the doc said.

"It might," Fargo conceded. "I still don't like the odds." Doc Schroder shrugged wearily, plainly resigned to whatever was about to happen.

Desmond Kray came out of the inn and his darting eyes frowned at Amanda. "Get the hell inside and start sweeping up the place," he barked.

Fargo smiled as Amanda's eyes flashed. "Say something to Mr. Kray," he said, and Kray let out a harsh guffaw.

"You're feeling humorous this morning, Fargo," the man said and frowned back at Amanda. "Go ahead, say something," he urged sadistically and guffawed again.

"If you ever try to touch me again I'll cut your balls off, you stinking, rotten weasel," Amanda said quietly.

Fargo couldn't stop his laugh as he saw Kray's face stiffen and his jaw drop open, the darting eyes stopping long enough to blink. Amanda turned and walked back into the inn, and Fargo watched Kray pull his mouth closed. His face was still wreathed in shock as he walked away. Fargo turned to see Doc Schroder staring at him. "What in God's name happened, or are you a miracle worker?" the army doctor asked.

"No miracles," Fargo said. "Or maybe miracles can come in the damnedest ways." He left the physician staring after him as he walked to saddle the Ovaro. When he returned, the doctor had gone to his quarters and Amanda waited by the door of the inn.

"Please come back," she said. "I want to scream again."

"I want that, too," he said. "I'll come back but maybe not tonight. Wait. Pray. Keep wanting to scream." She nodded, rose on tiptoe, and he leaned down to taste her lips and then he was riding off, the Ovaro in a fast canter.

8

Thoughts raced through Fargo's mind as he rode, priorities sorting themselves out. There was little question about the first one. He had to reach Red Flower with his scalp intact. Then he had to convince her to help him. The first would be the trickiest, he concluded. Red Flower had come to him that night because she'd wanted to. Not for honor, she had said. Because she had wanted him and that was important. She had also admitted that she feared the prospect of an all-out conflict. All of which meant that she would listen to him.

The next question sprang up instantly. She would listen but how much would she help? Red Bull was her brother and she was a Cheyenne woman. Loyalty and tribal pride ran deep inside her. How deep did the roots go, he wondered. How much would she help? Or perhaps more true to the point, how much *could* she? We are all captives of our heritage, of the responses conditioned within us. Red Flower would be no different. Then he winced at the thought that rose to push at him. Perhaps there were things she did not know. Perhaps he had come seeking answers she couldn't give even if she were willing to give them.

He swore into the wind and the questions rode with him as he climbed the rolling hills as the sun moved in its inexorable orbit across the sky. The orange sphere had begun to sink behind the high peaks when he reached the large expanse of cottonwoods. He slowed in the dimness that quickly cloaked the forest, slowed further as the dimness turned into blackness where only slivers of moonlight penetrated the forest. But his nostrils finally drew in the scene of wood smoke, and he knew the Cheyenne camp lay directly ahead. He halted at a spot where the lowest branches of a pair of cottonwoods touched each other as if they were a couple linking arms. Marking the spot in his mind, he left the Ovaro there and went on alone.

The scent of the wood smoke grew stronger as he neared the camp. He halted and dropped to one knee. He could see the silent campsite at the edge of the trees, a single fire burning low in the center. Remembering that the sentries had dropped from the trees at him during his last visit, Fargo's eyes searched the low branches, moving carefully in a slow circle—a precautionary exercise. He didn't expect Cheyenne sentries would be in the trees during the night darkness. When he was satisfied there were none in the branches he brought his gaze down to the edges of the camp. His eyes had traveled another dozen or so feet along the tree line when he spotted the sentry standing motionless against a tree trunk.

The Cheyenne wasn't wasting effort trying to peer into the blackness of the forest. He was standing motionless, letting his ears be his eyes, listening for any foreign sound out of the forest. Fargo let his eyes continue to circle the nearest part of the camp. There were other sentries, he was certain, but he grew convinced there were no more at this section of the camp, and he returned his eyes to the figure in front of him. He risked edging a few steps closer, moving on steps silent as those of a mountain lion. Pausing again, he drew the double-edged throwing knife from its sheath around his calf. He raised the blade, took aim, and in one motion he rose and lunged forward.

The Cheyenne heard the sound at once and spun around. But Fargo had already sent the blade hurtling through the dark. It imbedded itself into the base of the man's throat before he saw it, and Fargo saw him clasp his hand helplessly at the hilt of the knife as he began to fall. Fargo took another two long strides and reached the man in time to stop his body from thudding onto the ground. He pulled the lifeless form into the trees, retrieved the throwing knife, and wiped it clean on the grass before he began to crawl forward toward the silent, sleeping camp.

He saw some twenty sleeping forms scattered around the campsite, all braves, and another ten or so near the back edge of the camp. The others were in the tipis, and Fargo grimaced as he inched his way toward the tipi from which he had seen Red Flower emerge. Progress was slow, a pause after each few inches to glance around and be sure no one had woken. When he reached the edge of the tipi he felt his palms perspiring and he wiped them dry on the grass. The front flap of the tipi lay partially open, and Fargo, lying prone, inched his head through the opening. He held in the sigh of relief that welled up inside him. As he had dared to hope, there was only one figure asleep in the tipi. As the sister of the great warrior chief, Red Flower had her own tipi.

Fargo paused to glance up and back across the camp. It was still a sleeping place, but he cursed silently as he saw the first streaks of pink across the distant sky. He crawled into the tipi, where a low flame in a stone bowl kept the interior from being pitch black. He rose, took the small few steps on his feet, and looked down at the Indian girl as she lay with a wispy piece of cloth across her lovely breasts.

He placed one hand over her mouth and her eyes snapped open, stared up at him, and it took a moment for the panic to fade from her gaze. He lifted his hand from her mouth and she sat up, the wisp of cloth falling from the very round, perfectly placed breasts. "What are you doing here?" she breathed, her black-brown eyes round with wonder. "You will be killed if they catch you this time."

"I had to see you," Fargo said, and her eyes searched his face.

"Red Flower make you want her again?" she said.

"I want to know why you lied to me," Fargo said, and a small furrow slid across the young woman's smooth forehead. "About the woman. She was here. You lied to me."

The furrow became a frown. "I do not lie to you," she said.

He seized her wrists and shook her, a quick, hard gesture. "I saw the ribbon, on one of the women," Fargo hissed. "Red Bull lied to me. You lied to me. She was taken."

Fargo saw anger come into the young woman's face, her lovely jaw setting stubbornly. "My brother did not lie to you. He did not capture your woman. I did not lie."

"The squaw wore a piece of her clothes," Fargo flung back, his words accusing.

Red Flower's black-brown eyes smoldered. "I came to you. I would not lie to you," she said, her voice filled with reproach.

"Red Bull lied. He knew the woman I seek was here," Fargo said.

The Cheyenne girl looked away from him, her face tight. "My brother did not lie to you. He did not capture the woman," she said with dogged persistence. "That is what he told you. He did not lie."

Fargo damned her loyalty as her words circled inside him. She refused to budge. He hadn't been able to break through that tribal wall. The roots were too deep. Her insistence continued to circle through his mind and suddenly he felt his breath draw in sharply. He took her by the shoulders and pulled her around to face him. "Say it again," he demanded. "Let me hear you say it again."

"He did not capture your woman," she said, defiance in her eyes.

Damn, Fargo swore inwardly. He hadn't listened. He hadn't paid attention. They hadn't played word games. It hadn't been a matter of semantics. The Indians used words very specifically. Words were not lightly used. Each had its very own meaning. His hands stayed on the girl's shoulders. "He did not capture the woman. He did not take her as a captive is taken in a raid. He found her. He came upon her," Fargo said. Red Flower made no reply and her silence was an admission. "He found her but he took her. He did not capture her but he brought her here." The anger and defiance went out of the young girl's eyes.

"You must go. It is dawn. Others will be here," she said, her hands coming up to touch his face.

"He has her. He has her somewhere. He hides her. Why?" Fargo asked, excitement spiraling inside him.

The stubbornness was sliding into her face again when he heard the voices from outside, the camp waking. She clung to him for a moment. "Go, please go. There is no time. Go or they will kill you," she whispered, pressing her round breasts against him. She was right, he knew. There was no time. Perhaps he had already delayed too long. The voices outside were growing in numbers. She bent down, lifted the edge of the tipi at the rear. "This way. There are trees just beyond," she said.

Fargo dropped to his stomach, slid under the edge of the tent, and pushed himself along the ground. The camp was waking rapidly behind him as he crawled toward the stand of red ash at the rear of the encampment. He craned his neck to cast a glance behind, and glimpsing three braves cross on the other side of the tipi, he crawled as fast as he could. He was breathing hard when he reached the trees, more from tension than effort, and he stayed on his stomach as he moved inside the trees. The sun was up now, sliding across the camp as Fargo turned and rose to one knee. He saw Red Flower move away from the front of the tipi and then he glimpsed Red Bull as the chief marched across the center of the camp.

Fargo let a deep breath escape him. He hadn't the final answers he'd come to get, but he still had his scalp. He was lucky for that, he realized, and his glance scanned the edges of the camp. He'd have to lay low where he was, he decided, at least until he saw a moment to move in relative safety. He was still surveying his chances when he heard the sound rise in the morning air, grow stronger, become the rumble of unshod pony hoofs. He was frowning as the riders came into view and he saw them draw up before Red Bull, a young buck with a beaded arm band and a carbine in one hand leading the others. Fargo counted . . . ten, twenty, thirty, forty braves, all wearing war paint.

As he watched, he saw another band of riders arrive, these from west of the camp, twenty in all, and they, too, halted before Red Bull. All of the new arrivals dismounted at a sign from the chief. With his own braves joining, they sat in a circle around Red Bull. It was the beginning of a war council. Red Bull would lay out his plans, invoke the protection of the great warrior spirits, and the bloodshed would begin.

It was also Fargo's chance to get away. Everyone, including the sentries, was taking part in the war council. Fargo rose to his feet and began to circle the camp, forcing himself to move slowly and silently. A wrong step, an unexpected sound, and they'd break off their council instantly. He drew deeper into the trees, continued to circle and move with infuriating slowness.

He reached the cottonwoods and turned into the forest. He had to reach Cogswell. The captain would be outnumbered by more than two to one, now. His only chance was to draw back to the barracks and make the Cheyenne attack him in a defensible position. Fargo's lips were a tight line when he finally reached the two cottonwoods where he'd left the Ovaro. He swung into the saddle, started to wheel the horse around, then paused and listened. The sound came to him again, the soft hooves of unshod ponies. The Cheyenne were on the move. The war council had been a short one, the spirits invoked without the usual ceremonies.

That meant two things. The new arrivals were already familiar with Red Bull's plans and the Cheyenne chief was so confident he didn't feel the need to invoke the full strength of the warrior spirits. Fargo put the Ovaro into a fast trot, skirting trees until he was out of the cottonwoods, where he sent the horse into a full gallop. He rode hard and drew to a halt on a ridge behind a cover of spruce. He swept the terrain behind and below and saw the Cheyenne force, Red Bull in the lead, moving northward at a steady trot. Some carried army carbines, but most bows and lances. He sent the Ovaro into a trot, staying ahead of the Cheyenne and in tree cover where he could watch them as they rode. They stayed mostly on the lowland, choosing cuts and ravines rather than hills, but their direction remained north. It was when they reached a long, low stretch of land between two hills that Fargo saw Red Bull wave commands with his arm, and the main band of riders behind him broke off into two groups of about fifty warriors each.

One group began to climb the far hill and the other started toward the hill where he rode. Fargo put the Ovaro into a fast canter, staying in tree cover, and raced on. He had seen enough. The Cheyenne chief intended a three-pronged strike with himself leading the band to face Cogswell. Fargo emerged from the other side of the trees and sent the pinto into a gallop. He desperately hoped that Cogswell hadn't taken the field yet. His hope was shattered when he caught the plume of dust ahead. He raced the horse down a gentle slope, up the other side, and came into sight of the long column of blue-and-gold uniforms.

"Damn," Fargo swore as he raced forward and saw the captain wave his troop to a halt. The young lieutenant flanked Cogswell on one side and Doc Schroder on the other. The captain fastened Fargo with a coolly amused smile.

"Still turning up at unexpected times, I see," Cogswell said.

"Still trying to save your ass," Fargo bit out. "The Cheyenne are on the other sides of those hills, moving this way through a wide ravine."

"Perfect," Cogswell smiled confidently.

"Three columns of some fifty each," Fargo said. "They're going to hit you from three sides and you're outnumbered three to one."

Cogswell offered a deprecating grin. "You wouldn't be trying to get me to turn back, would you, Fargo?" he asked.

"Yes, Goddammit, while you're all alive and able to ride," Fargo threw at him.

Cogswell turned in the saddle. "Corporal Dent, take one man and ride out. Report back to me the minute you see anything," he ordered and Fargo watched the two soldiers race away and disappear over the hill.

"You really think I made this up?" Fargo frowned at the captain.

"I think you're not above exaggerating. I think you'd do anything to make me look bad. I think you're afraid of the Cheyenne," Cogswell said. "Does that answer you?" Fargo nodded, his eyes suddenly a steel blue. "Dismount," Cogswell ordered his men. "We'll have a twenty-minute wait, I'd guess." The troop dismounted. Fargo stayed in the saddle and saw the uncertain glances exchanged by some of the men. It was apparent that they were nervous and less than completely confident in the captain. Some of the men sat cross-legged beside their horses and he saw the beefy-faced sergeant and the other two standing together, their eyes still averting his direct stare. The captain's guess as to time proved accurate enough when the two troopers finally reappeared. "Mount up," Cogswell ordered as the two men rode to a halt in front of him.

"Cheyenne, sir. They're coming, all right," the corporal said.

"How many?" Cogswell asked.

"One column. I'd guess about fifty," the trooper said.

"The others went into the hills flanking them," Fargo interjected.

"You check the hills, Corporal?" Cogswell questioned.

"We didn't ride into them but we surveyed them," the soldier said. "Looked real hard, too. We didn't see any signs of riders."

Fargo groaned and knew what had happened. The

two Cheyenne bands had dismounted and were moving forward spaced out and single file. They'd avoided the high profile of a man on horseback. "There are two more columns, dammit," Fargo barked. "Believe me." Cogswell's answer was a tolerant smile. "You're going to get yourself and everyone else killed," Fargo shouted.

Cogswell's face darkened. "You're under arrest, mister," he snapped. "Take his gun, Corporal." Two troopers came up to flank Fargo at once and he felt the Colt being lifted from its holster.

"What's the charge?" Fargo growled.

"I'll think of something. Giving false information to a United States Army officer in pursuit of hostiles. That'll do for now," Cogswell said. "I'm just tired of your damn interference."

"You fool. You poor fool," Fargo said and felt as much overwhelming sadness as he did anger.

"Tie his hands and take him back to the barracks. Put him in the guardhouse," the captain said.

"You can't spare two men to take me all the way back," Fargo said.

Cogswell returned a narrow-eyed, thoughtful stare. "Perhaps not," he agreed and turned to the beefy-faced sergeant. "Take him high into the hills. Tie him to a tree. You'll come back for him after it's over," Cogswell ordered.

The sergeant rode up with a length of rope and tied Fargo's wrists in front of him so he could hold onto the saddle horn. Cogswell brought his mount a few steps closer. "But you have given me an idea, Fargo. I'm going to turn back and let the Cheyenne think we've decided to retreat instead of fight. They'll come after us, of course, and when I'm at the right spot, I'll turn and attack," he said, wheeled the horse around and moved the column on. Fargo watched him lead his men south at a slow trot and then the beefy-faced sergeant and a younger trooper were flanking him, starting up the nearest hill with him.

They rode slowly, climbing the first hill and through a thicket of hawthorn and then starting up another hill beyond it. Fargo's thoughts raced wildly. There was but one slender chance left. If he could somehow bring Arlene back in time to prevent the massacre. If things went perfectly, there was still time. Cogswell would draw the Cheyenne as far south as he could before turning to fight and he'd want to find the right spot to make a proper stand. That would all take time. There was still a chance left. But that meant finding Arlene, and Red Flower was the only way to do that. If, indeed, she knew, Fargo reminded himself grimly. But it was the only chance he had left.

The troopers had crested the top of the second hill with him and they drew to a halt where a dozen black oak rose. "This'll do," the beefy-faced sergeant said. "Get off your horse," he ordered Fargo.

"Don't make the ropes too tight. Give me a chance to work them loose by dark," Fargo said. "You don't want to leave me here for the wolves, do you?"

"We'll be back for you," the sergeant said.

"No," Fargo said sadly. "You won't be back for me. Nobody will."

"Cut out that kind of talk, damn you," the sergeant said and Fargo saw the moment of fear pass through the man's face.

"I'm right, like it or not," Fargo said. "I'll make a deal with you. If I show you the other Cheyenne columns you let me go."

The man frowned, uncertainty in his face. "What then?" he asked.

"You can ride off and save your necks or you can go tell Cogswell you saw the other Cheyenne. Maybe he'll listen to you," Fargo said. "You leave me and ride back and you're dead men." He watched the sergeant exchange glances with the other trooper.

"It's a deal," the sergeant said. "I owe you one."

Fargo nodded, wanting to tell the man he hadn't reported him out of sympathy and deciding against it. This was not the time for explaining motives. He stayed silent and the man untied his wrist bonds. "Stay with me," Fargo said and sent the Ovaro into a gallop. He turned south and rode higher, onto a long ridge, crossed down and over another, and the Cheyenne led by Red Bull came into view along the flatland. Fargo reined to a halt, and his eyes swept the hills on both sides, fastening at a spot where the trees thinned along the far ridge. "There . . . keep your eyes there," he said and pointed with one arm.

The two troopers followed his directions, and Fargo saw the Cheyenne on the high ground flick by, on their ponies now, but still riding single file. One came into view for an instant, then seconds later, another and another and a seemingly endless procession of flicking shapes. "Jesus," the young trooper breathed.

"Now look over at that other ridge, right in the center where the hackberry dip down," Fargo said and fastened his own eyes at the spot as the second band of Cheyenne moved by, riding east in pairs. "Holy shit," the trooper murmured.

"Your shot," Fargo said and put the Ovaro into a gallop. He glanced back as he raced away and saw the two men trying to decide what they should do. Fargo returned to his riding. It didn't much matter what they decided, he knew. If they left to save their own skins the captain would be two men short, almost meaningless now. And if they returned, Cogswell wouldn't listen to them. He wouldn't flee. He was too consumed with his own obsession to do anything but fight. Fargo drew his lips back in bitterness as he raced the pinto through a narrow defile that he had spotted a few days back.

He reached the cottonwood forest and kept the horse going full-out. There was neither need nor time for caution. The Ovaro swerved, turned, and skirted trees, hardly slowing, as only he could, and suddenly Fargo saw the Cheyenne camp in front of him. He charged into the camp and saw squaws scatter to all sides. Two old men tried to rush at him with lances but he swerved the horse and sent them both flying to the ground. He came to a halt in front of the tipi as they landed on their backs, and Red Flower came out, her eyes wide more with surprise than fright. He leaned down, scooped her up in one arm and threw her onto the saddle in front of him. He raced from the camp as another old man flung a lance that missed with feet so spare. He stopped when he'd ridden another thousand feet into the cottonwoods.

"Where is she?" he barked at Red Flower. "The killing will begin soon, very soon."

"The Cheyenne will win," she said truculently.

"Maybe, but many will die. Even if the Cheyenne win they will lose many fine young braves," Fargo said. "Red Bull may die. The bluecoat soldiers are trained warriors, too." She stared back at him but he saw her eyes flicker. "We can stop the killing. You can help me stop it. You do not want Red Bull to die." Her eyes looked away and he saw the flash of concern touch her face. "You know where the woman is. Take me to her. That's the only way to stop the killing. Now. There is no time left. It may already be too late."

She brought her eyes back to his. "There are guards," she said.

"I may have to kill them. I don't know. Take me,"

he insisted. She thought for a moment more and then nodded and gestured west through the trees. He put the pinto into a fast canter and followed her directions as she rode soundlessly with him, using only her hands to point the way. She had him turn further west and ride up a hillside still covered with the cottonwoods. Partway up the slope she put a hand on his arm.

"Stop here," she said, and he halted and let her slide from the saddle before swinging to the ground to stand beside him. "Through there," she said, indicating a dense growth of red ash mingling with the cottonwoods. He gestured and she led the way as he followed close behind her. The slope leveled off slightly and the red ash thinned enough for him to see the cave entrance and the two Cheyenne sentries outside it, both clad only in breechclouts and both holding carbines. Red Flower shot a glance at him and he motioned for her to go forward as he dropped to one knee. He drew the double-edged throwing knife from its calf holster as he watched the two sentries come alert, rifles instantly raised as they heard Red Flower approach.

She stepped from the trees and Fargo moved another dozen paces closer. Recognizing her, the two braves lowered their guns as she spoke to them. Fargo heard her tone, crisp, commanding befitting the sister of their chief. One brave stepped back in deference but the other planted himself in front of the cave entrance and blocked her way. Red Flower's voice grew angry and Fargo heard her demand. "Out of my way. I have come for the woman," she said.

But the brave was stubborn. "Only Red Bull," he insisted. She turned to the other one

"Tell him to move away," she said but the other Indian only shrugged his shoulders, plainly uncertain what to do. Red Flower turned back to the figure blocking the face entrance. "You will be sorry," she said.

"Only Red Bull," the man repeated again. Fargo swore silently. Every damn second was precious. There was no more time for arguing. He flung the blade, a short, powerful movement of his arm, all the strength of his shoulders behind it. He saw the blade hurtle past Red Flower's shoulder and slam into the Indian's abdomen. The man dropped his gun, doubled over, and grabbed at his midsection, and the second sentry whirled around to bring his gun up. Fargo saw Red Flower spin and try to seize the man's gun, and as she wrestled over the weapon he dug his heels into the soft ground and charged from the trees. The brave had just yanked his gun free and flung the girl aside when Fargo hurled himself at him. He tried to bring the carbine around but Fargo's looping left caught him on the point of the jaw. He staggered back, still hanging onto the gun. Fargo's follow-through right smashed into the same spot on his jaw. He went down and the gun dropped from his hands.

"Take the gun," Fargo told Red Flower, and she picked up the weapon as he ran into the cave to see the figure tied hand and foot and huddled against the wall. He bent down and untied her ankle ropes first. "You're getting out of here," he said.

"Oh, God, oh, thank God," Arlene Kelly said, and he lifted her to her feet and walked her from the cave. Outside, he saw that she seemed not to have been mistreated and she looked very much as she did in the tintype, dark brown hair still braided and tight around her face. He retrieved the knife and cut her wrist bonds.

"Fargo," he said. "Skye Fargo."

Arlene stared at him with eyes round with gratitude.

"You don't know how glad I am to see you," she said. "How did you ever find me?"

He pointed to Red Flower and the young woman looked at her with surprise. "But she is Red Bull's sister," Arlene said.

"That's right. And before her, Amanda helped me," Fargo said. "It's a long story and I need you to fill in some very important details. But time's important. I don't want to stand around talking. We've got to find a horse for you."

"These two have their ponies behind the cave," Arlene said. Red Flower strode away instantly, not waiting for him to tell her, and returned in moments leading two sturdy ponies, one fitted with only a saddle blanket, the other wearing an elkhorn saddle over a blanket. Red Flower pulled herself onto the pony with only the blanket, leaving the other for Arlene, and Fargo caught the faint air of superiority that touched her face. He gave Arlene a helping hand onto the elkhorn saddle and swung onto the Ovaro.

"Let's go. We can talk while we ride," he said, and the two young women fell in on both sides of him as he led the way down the hill. "You ran away. Amanda told me that much. You were running when the Cheyenne came upon you. Is that right?"

"That's right," Arlene said.

"They didn't purposely come after you," Fargo said.

"No, I was running on my own," Arlene said.

"Why?" Fargo questioned as they emerged from the cottonwoods.

"I was running away from Desmond Kray. I'd found out something, and he knew I'd found it out. I was afraid he'd kill me if I stayed. I'm sure he would have," Arlene said.

"What was it you learned?" Fargo asked.

"That Kray had been selling rifles to the Cheyenne, to Red Bull," Arlene said. "I couldn't sleep one night and went outside. I saw Desmond Kray arguing with the man he used as a contact, a half-breed I saw visit the trading post regularly."

"Why were they arguing?"

"Red Bull was furious. The ammunition Kray sold them for the rifles was no good. Red Bull demanded Kray supply him with good ammunition or return all the pelts that had been traded for the rifles."

"And Kray wasn't about to do either," Fargo said.

"He was sending back half-promises, being tricky again. When the half-breed left, Kray started back to the house. I ran inside but I dropped a shawl I'd taken with me. I didn't realize it till I was back in my room."

"But Kray found it and put two and two together. It added up to you having overheard," Fargo said.

"Yes. He kept watching me all the next day, asking questions, probing. I knew then I had to run. There was nothing else to do. I couldn't even go to the captain. He was away," Arlene said. "So that night I packed my things and ran."

"That's when Red Bull came upon you."

"The next morning. He and a dozen of his men were riding and found me. The half-breed was with him and recognized who I was at once. He told Red Bull. Later he told me that I was being held to force Kray to give back the pelts or good ammunition," Arlene said. She paused and a note of bitterness came into her voice. "They thought that Desmond Kray cared about me, his niece, and he'd agree to get me back safe. That was certainly a mistake."

"Instead, Kray saw his chance. He told Cogswell the Cheyenne had kidnapped you and it was time to wipe out Red Bull. That fed perfectly into Cogswell's own ambitions. It gave him the final excuse he needed to start an all-out war," Fargo said.

"How very neat for Desmond," Arlene said. "If he doesn't ransom me by returning their pelts, the Cheyenne will kill me. That takes care of me. Then he gets the captain to wipe out the Cheyenne and that takes care of Red Bull and there's nobody left to know he sold guns to the Indians."

"You were being used as a pawn by everybody. The Cheyenne used you to try to get to Kray. Kray used you to get to Cogswell, and the captain used you as an excuse to start an all-out war with the Cheyenne," Fargo said.

"Desmond Kray won't be getting his way now," Arlene said.

"Don't be too sure of that," Fargo said, and the young woman shot a frowning glance at him. "If we don't stop the battle and Red Bull is killed, Kray won't have to worry about him. If Cogswell's killed, too, he'll be completely in the clear. It'll just be your word and you can't prove anything and there'll be nobody to prove it to."

"I'll take up where I left off . . . running," the young woman said.

"That makes it more important than ever to stop the killing before it starts. That's why you're both here. Cogswell will listen to you and Red Bull will listen to his sister," Fargo said. "After Cogswell sees you alive and hears how Kray used him and Red Flower tells her brother how Kray whipped up Cogswell to kill him, I'm thinking that'll be enough to make them both back off."

Arlene fell silent and he glanced at the young Indian girl. Red Flower's lovely face was set tightly. She had understood none of the conversation he'd had with Arlene, but it didn't matter. She understood why she rode here beside him. She cared nothing about Arlene or Kray or Cogswell. She cared nothing about the thirst for battle of young bucks, for tribal vengeance, for Red Bull's pride in leadership. She cared only about the terrible price of victory. She cared only about the death of the brother she loved. That was enough.

Fargo kept the Ovaro at a full gallop, aware that the real enemy now was time. But perhaps that had always been the real enemy.

9

Hope shattered riding up a long slope, and desperate dreams tore apart with the roll of sound. Fargo felt despair sweep through him as the deep staccato bark of rifle fire resounded, punctuated by the lighter, crisper crack of revolver shots. "Goddamn," he spit out and both young women flashed quick glances of alarm at him. "We're too late. They're into it, full into it," he said, and as if in answer the deep, heavy boom rolled through the air. The captain was still using his dynamite.

Fargo raced forward and crested the top of the slope a few yards in front of the two young women. He halted, saw one more low hill ahead, the battle going on beyond the second hill. He sent the Ovaro galloping and the sounds grew louder, war whoops, high and shrill, rising over the sound of the gunfire. He was a dozen yards ahead of the two other horses as he charged upward, the battle noises close now, and he slowed as he topped the hill, reined to a stop, and saw the high plain stretched out in front of him. Low rock and some tree cover bordered both sides of the plain with low hills rising at both edges.

In between, across the flatland, bodies littered the ground almost from side to side. As many wore uniforms as wore breechclouts and leggings, and Fargo heard the double gasp of dismay as Arlene and Red Flower came up alongside him. Fargo's eyes took in more than the field littered with the dead. He saw the details that told him what had taken place. Cogswell's men were hunkered down behind a low rock formation, but it was obvious they hadn't taken cover fast enough. Instead, they had attacked Red Bull's column head-on and found themselves attacked from both sides, caught in a three-way pincer. Cogswell had fled to the rock cover then but he'd already lost heavily.

The Cheyenne had been overeager in pursuing an immediate charge. From the way their slain warriors were clustered they had been met by Cogswell's dynamite sticks. But now the Cheyenne had drawn back into a main force that faced the troopers behind the rocks. However, a smaller force had circled around to a hill behind the troopers, from which vantage point they hurled arrows and some rifle fire down onto the rocks. They were there to keep part of Cogswell's men ducking arrows and firing back and to reduce the numbers available to counter Red Bull's main force. As Fargo watched, he saw three small bands of Cheyenne race across the flatland at the troops.

The Cheyenne raced head-on toward the rocks, fired off a volley of arrows and rifle fire, and peeled off. They circled, charged again, and peeled off again. They were covering their feints with firepower, plainly trying to see if Cogswell's men still had dynamite to throw. After the third and closest charge they peeled off again and returned to the main force in the tree cover. The troopers had been too busy ducking arrows to return much fire, but there had been no more dynamite thrown. Cogswell had only a half-dozen sticks, Fargo recalled. It was likely he had no more left. Something else was even more likely. Once Red Bull decided his enemy was out of his main weapon, he would charge, directly, from the sides and from behind the rocks. He would suffer the losses. There was glory in losses, in death. Destroying the enemy was all that mattered.

But the Cheyenne chief would never know that the glory was not really all his. He had to share that with a man named Burton Cogswell. Blind, ruthless ambition and implacable, ruthless hate had combined to produce an orgy of death, all of it brought together by one wolf-faced rotten little man. "No," Fargo said, uttering the word aloud. "No, Goddamm it." He was here. He wasn't going to sit by and watch in helpless frustration. He hadn't come this far without one last try. He glanced at Arlene, then at the Cheyenne girl. "One of you on each side of me. Stay low in the saddle and watch me. When I sit up you sit up. Till then, stay close at a fast canter," he said. Arlene nodded and he spoke to Red Flower. "With me. Follow me," he said with a sign and she also nodded.

He sent the Ovaro into a fast canter, saw both young women stay alongside him, their legs touching his. They bent low across their mounts as he pushed himself flat on the Ovaro, and he sent the horse straight across the flat plain. He kept at the fast canter, riding through the arrows and rifle shots that were whistling from both sides. He was directly in the center, between the troopers and the Cheyenne when he sat up in the saddle and saw Arlene and Red Flower do the same. He reined to a halt and heard the rifle fire sputter to a stop. A half-dozen arrows dropped to the ground nearby. He cast a glance at the Cheyenne and caught a glimpse of Red Bull's powerful, bare-chested figure among the others lined up to charge.

"Stay right where you are," he muttered to the two

young women. "Sit tall. Let them all see you." He waited and drew in the silence that had fallen over the scene. He let his horse move two steps forward as he lifted his voice. "Captain Cogswell, come out here," he called. Turning, he spoke in Algonquian. "Is the mighty Red Bull afraid to come to me?" he asked and fell silent. He realized the palms of his hands were wet and he wiped them dry on his trousers. The blue-uniformed figure detached itself from the rocks and came forward on foot and he looked toward the massed riders. Slowly, Red Bull moved out into the open astride his grayish-white pony. But the uniformed figure neared first and he saw the young face of Lieutenant Wilson, a red scrape on his forehead that matched his red hair. "Where's the captain?" Fargo asked.

"Killed, sir, in the first charge," the lieutenant said.

"Captain Schroder?"

"Treating the wounded. He said as ranking field officer I was in charge," Wilson said.

Fargo turned to the Indian chief as the man halted a few feet from him. "Tell him how Kray wanted the soldiers to kill him," Fargo said to Red Flower. "Tell him that Arlene meant nothing to Kray." Red Flower spoke quickly to her brother. When she finished, the Indian's face remained impassive. But his eyes were bits of black fire when he turned to Fargo.

"She is important to you," the Indian said. "My warriors attack and every soldier dies. The woman, too."

"Red Flower, too," Fargo said. He met the chief's angry eyes with cold blue steel in his own. Red Flower's voice broke into the silent tension, her words quick, her voice tight. He caught only a little of what she said to her brother. Red Bull's face remained impassive but his voice grew less harsh.

"My sister says too many have died here," the Cheyenne chief said. "She asks if I want to see her die, too." Fargo held his own face impassive and let his silence answer. The Indian took another long moment to speak again. "We will take our dead," he said, finally.

Fargo nodded and spoke to the lieutenant. "Start putting your dead and wounded on their mounts," he said. "Take this young lady to your lines." Wilson nodded, grasped Arlene's horse by the halter, and started back to the rocks. Fargo closed a hand over Red Flower's arm and took her to one side with him as he watched the Cheyenne begin to gather up their dead. He felt the bitter irony inside himself as he saw the lieutenant's men moving almost side by side with the Cheyenne as they retrieved the slain troopers.

Finally it was finished and Fargo moved forward with Red Flower to where the Cheyenne chief sat his pony. "The bluecoats lose many," the Indian said, a note of contempt in his voice.

"More soldiers will be sent," Fargo said.

"More Cheyenne will come to fight with Red Bull," the Indian said. "It is finished here, now. But it is not over."

Fargo heard the grimness of his own voice as he knew the only answer was an echo. "No it is not over," he said and the Cheyenne chief turned his horse and rode slowly away. Fargo's eyes sought out the slender figure that still waited beside him. She met his gaze but her black-brown orbs spoke their own words. She told him in silence that shared bodies and shared concerns neither last nor change the way of things. Deeds had been repaid, balances met, she was still a Cheyenne, and he was still an intruder. He watched her walk her pony after her brother and disappear into the distance with the rest of the near-naked riders.

Fargo turned and walked the pinto to where the lieutenant waited, Arlene beside him, the dead and the wounded in a long column behind him. "We'd all be dead if it weren't for you. I want you to know that I know that, sir," Wilson said.

"Send for replacements soon as you get back, son. Nothing's really changed," Fargo said.

"Miss Arlene told me about Desmond Kray. I'll arrest him soon as we get back," the lieutenant said and waved the column forward. Fargo dropped back and found Doc Schroder at the rear of the wounded, his face strained and fatigued.

"You were right all along," the army doctor said. "Cogswell paid the price for not listening to you. I know you don't take any satisfaction in that, but he was willing to risk the life of every man here for his own ends. Maybe justice works in its own ways."

"Maybe," Fargo allowed and rode in silence beside the doctor on the long, slow return. Dusk was beginning to settle when they reached the barracks. Amanda flew from the inn and searched the line for him. He swung from the saddle and was on the ground as she reached him and flew into his arms, her mouth wet and hot against his.

"You've come back. Oh, God, I was so afraid," she murmured, and he walked back to where Arlene had dismounted with her and enjoyed the total surprise in Arlene's face as Amanda spoke to her. They were still talking when the lieutenant returned.

"Kray's not here. He's gone, taken his horse and gear with him and left his woman," Wilson said.

"Traveling hard and fast," Fargo said. "Why'd he light out?"

"I think I can answer that," Amanda said. "After the captain left with everyone he waited for about an hour and then rode off in the same direction."

"He followed us," the lieutenant said.

"He stayed back but close enough to see for himself what happened," Fargo said. "He had to see me arrive with Arlene and he knew the jig was up. He raced back here, got his gear, and ran."

"I've no men in any shape to go after him," Wilson said.

"Write him off, lieutenant. He's not the only polecat that's outrun the law and his crimes," Fargo said.

"Nevertheless, I'll have headquarters send out wanted posters on him to every sheriff in the West. Maybe we'll still nail him," Wilson said and strode away. Fargo turned to see Arlene with her arm around Amanda.

"We've so much to talk about," she said.

"Yes," Amanda said, but Fargo saw her eyes were on him. "We have to talk, too," she said. "In the morning. You must be exhausted now."

"That's about it," he conceded. "In the morning." Amanda nodded gravely but he saw the tiny lights in her eyes, their own silent messages. She hadn't stopped sending wordless messages, he thought, smiling inwardly, and he went to his room, shed his clothes, and fell across the cot. He was asleep in seconds.

He slept later than he usually did and when he was finally washed and dressed he went outside to see Amanda in the pale yellow dress. She rushed into his arms at once. "You and Arlene do all your catching up last night?" he asked, and she nodded into his chest before she stepped back.

"Arlene's going to stay for a while," Amanda said. "She mostly ran the place when Kray was here. She can do it for herself, make some money, and then leave."

"Sounds fair enough," Fargo said. "What about Amanda?"

"I have relatives in Wyoming, near Casper. I'll go there but not until . . ." Amanda said, her eyes dancing again.

"Not until what?" he asked.

"Not until you make me scream again, night after night," she said, and her arms were around him, her lips against his. "You promised," she murmured.

"I'll take you to Casper, the long way," he said. "Pack. The lieutenant will give me an army mount for you."

She flew from him with quick, graceful steps and he went to the barracks. Wilson was there with Doc Schroder. "For you, Fargo, a dozen mounts if you want them," the lieutenant said.

"One will do." Fargo smiled as the lieutenant went off to get the horse.

"You going to give that young lady more of that miracle treatment that got her talking?" Doc Schroder said, his eyes twinkling.

"Count on it," Fargo said and took the bay army mount the lieutenant brought back. "Good luck to you both," he said.

"And to you," the lieutenant said. Amanda appeared with her few things pushed into a sack and tied it behind the cantle. Arlene came out to stand beside Doc Schroder and the lieutenant. Fargo rode from the barracks with Amanda beside him and knew he could feel no more than a limited kind of satisfaction. Complete disaster had been avoided, a full-scale uprising had been turned aside, but only for now. The hate and the power remained. Nothing had been ended, only deferred. The Cheyenne chief's words rode with him. It was not over. But others would take it up, at other times and in other places. Amanda's voice cut into his thoughts.

"You're thinking real hard. About what?" she asked.

"Sorry," he said. "It's not important anymore, not to you or to me." He reached out, pulled her to him and let his lips find hers. "This is all I'm going to be thinking about from now on," he said and led the way down a narrow gorge that brought them to a deep valley of sweet cicely as dusk descended. The night stayed warm enough so there was no need for anything but a blanket. It grew a lot warmer as Amanda came to him in all her naked loveliness, her perfectly shaped, milk-white breasts beckoning his touch. She gently pressed the delicate pink, flat, virginal tips to his mouth and pressed him down on the blanket.

He took first one, then the other, and there was no silence this time as Amanda cried out, gasped, purred, and groaned at his every touch. His hands explored all her sweet curves, all the dark places he had explored that first night, but now there was no more silent tossing, no more holding back the sounds of ecstasy. "Yes, yes, yes . . . oh, yes," she breathed at his every caress. "More, more, oh, God, more." When he rose with her, exploded with her, and joined in her final pleasure, Amanda's shriek rent the warm night, a cry as primeval as that shrieked by the very first woman that very first moment.

When she fell back onto the blanket, clasping him to her, she quivered in his arms and covered his face with quick kisses. It was later, when he lay beside her and the moon rose higher, that he felt her hands touch his, move down his muscled body, across his chest, down his thigh and back up to his abdomen. Her hands made little fluttery motions and her quick gasps were an echo and he felt himself rising to her touch. When her fingers closed around his pulsing, throbbing warmth, Amanda's mouth opened and she half screamed, a sound of pure, sensual delight. She clasped harder, stroked, turned, caressed, her hands exploring, absorbing touch, feel, sensation. He felt her long, lovely thighs fall open, and she came over him, pressed down on him, pushed her wet warmth over him as she fell forward, her breasts against his face. Her half-screams of delight became long cries of ecstasy as she clasped him tightly, rising up and down and thrust back and forth, absorbing all of him into her warmth until he felt her tightening around him. His own body responded, pulsations bursting with her, and he held her quivering body tight against him until, with a half-sob, she went limp and lay atop him. Tiny sounds of contentment escaped her parted lips.

She slept with him through the warm night and woke only when the sun bathed her back in its yellow glow. "As wonderful as the first time, maybe more wonderful," she murmured as he rose with her. "And I will wait all day for the night."

"Maybe you won't have to wait till night," Fargo said.

"Good," she said happily, her face wreathed in instant anticipation. When they began to ride, after breakfasting on a cluster of wild plums he found, he set a leisurely pace through meandering pathways. The day turned hot and sticky and it was near the close of the afternoon that he came upon a deep pond, almost a small lake. The clear coolness of its water told him it was fed by underground well-springs. They shed their clothes and washed away the day's dust and perspiration in the cool water, and when they finished he enjoyed the shining beauty of Amanda as she stretched out to dry in the last rays of the sun.

A few droplets of water still glistened on her abdomen as she pressed herself down over him. "It's almost night," she murmured.

"Close enough," he agreed and closed his hands around the firm softness of her round little rear. He turned with her, stretched her onto her back, and found one lovely breast with his lips. Her soft moan came at once. "Aaaaah, yes, yes," she breathed, and her legs lifted, pressing against his ribs, and she held his mouth to her, both her hands clasped to his face. Amanda's soft moans grew in volume, sweet song of pleasure, when he heard the sound, foreign, intrusive, and unmistakable, the soft click of a trigger being cocked.

"Now isn't this a pretty picture," the voice said and Fargo fell away from Amanda as he turned to stare up at the figure standing a dozen paces away, revolver cocked and aimed.

"Kray," he spit out as he silently cursed himself. Complacency. Underestimation. Haste. They all came out the same way. He had misjudged Desmond Kray. He shouldn't have, he realized bitterly. The man had already shown his deviousness. Fargo's eyes flicked to where the Colt lay in its holster near the pond's edge, the throwing knife in its own calf-holster beside it.

"Don't even think about it," Kray's voice barked and he took three quick steps, scooped up the Colt, and stuck it into his belt. "Get dressed," he ordered and stepped back again as Fargo pulled on clothes. Amanda reached over and drew the yellow dress over herself. Kray seemed to pay little attention to her.

"Turn around," Kray ordered and Fargo, his lips a grim line, turned his back on the man. The crash of the gun butt against the top of his head was a sharp, instant pain and he was aware only of himself pitching forward as the world vanished.

His eyelids flickered when consciousness returned and he took a moment to remember and then to focus his vision. He was still lying on his face but he hadn't been there long, he was certain. The blow had been hard enough to knock him out but not hard enough to keep him unconscious for long. He lifted his head, pushed up on the palms of his hands, and came to his knees to see Amanda tightly bound against a tree and Kray standing nearby. A flicker of hope stirred inside Fargo. Kray didn't intend on killing them right away.

"What do you think you're going to do?" he asked Desmond Kray.

"I don't aim to spend the rest of my life running from sheriffs and bounty hunters," Kray said. "I figure the lieutenant's going to send out 'wanted' posters."

"He is," Fargo said.

"That little bitch niece of mine is the only one who can make a case against me. Without her he can send out all the fliers he wants. They won't mean shit," Kray said. "So I'm going to take care of little Arlene and you're going to help me."

"How?" Fargo frowned.

"Wilson may have sentries posted, probably does. I can't walk in and get the little bitch but you can and that's exactly what you're going to do," Kray said.

"And if I don't?"

"I put a bullet through your little girlfriend's head," Kray snarled. "You don't want that, do you?"

"No, I don't want that," Fargo said.

"Then get on your horse. We're going back to the inn, you and me, mister," Kray said. "When we get near enough, I'll stay back and you go in and get her. Nobody's going to question you."

"What if she won't come?" Fargo said.

"Tell her I just want her to sign a piece of paper saying she never saw or heard me dealing with the Cheyenne," Kray said.

"You think she's going to believe that?" Fargo sneered.

"You make her believe it," Kray said.

"What if I don't bother to come out with her?" Fargo said.

"I'm going to be holding your horse with me. You don't come out with her and I'll be back here long before you can get here. When you do you'll find this little piece real dead," Kray said. "One tricky move and you can count on it."

Fargo walked to the Ovaro. The man had planned well enough in his cunning way. There was nothing to do but play along with him for now. It would buy time, time to find a way out or time for Kray to grow lax. Time was again all-important. Fargo climbed onto the Ovaro, cast a glance at Amanda, who nodded back in understanding. Kray swung in behind him as Fargo started to retrace steps. "I figure we'll get there just before dawn," Kray said from behind him. "If you don't get smart. Then you won't get there at all and little Amanda's dead."

"That still leaves Arlene," Fargo reminded him.

"I'll have to figure out some other way to get to her. But right now this is the way," the man said. "You don't give me any trouble and I might just let you and little Amanda go. You don't know anything except what Arlene told you and that won't count for anything."

Riding behind him, Kray didn't see the grim smile that came to Fargo's lips. The offer was but another piece of bait tossed out. Kray had no intention of letting them ride away alive. But he wanted Arlene first. Fargo rode on in silence. He passed a half-dozen places where he considered making a dive for nearby heavy brush cover but he decided against it each time. Kray was too close to miss. If he got himself killed, Fargo knew, that meant Amanda's death, also. Time, he murmured to himself at each spot. He couldn't afford to hurry time now.

The moon was starting to slide toward the horizon when they came in sight of the dark, silent cluster of buildings that marked Kray's Corners and the barracks. "This is far enough," Kray ordered. "You walk from here." Fargo swung from the horse and glanced at Kray. The man had held the revolver directly at his back all the way and he didn't waver now, Fargo saw. He turned and began to walk toward the dark buildings. He crossed in front of the barracks, aware that he was well in sight of Kray's narrowed eyes, and he waved to the sentry as he crossed into the inn. Once inside, he hurried to the room and entered and saw Arlene sit up at once at the sound.

"It's me," he said quickly and she stifled her scream and swung from the bed, clothed in a long, white nightgown.

"What are you doing here?" Arlene asked.

"Command performance," he said and told her what had happened in quick, terse sentences.

"My God," Arlene breathed when he finished.

"I can't ask you to come," Fargo said. "But if you don't, Amanda's dead for sure. If you come with me, I'll have a little more time to get us all out alive. He won't shoot you anywhere near here where the shot could be heard."

"Maybe he just wants me to sign that piece of paper," Arlene offered.

Fargo made a harsh sound. "He can't leave you alive," he said. Arlene nodded gravely.

"I suppose not," she said. "You want to wait outside while I dress."

"Thanks," Fargo said.

"No thanks," Arlene told him. "I'd be dead if Amanda hadn't made you come looking for me. This is my chance to do the same for her."

Fargo nodded, stepped from the room, his hands clenched in tight, hammerlike fists. The last chance was coming up. He had to find some moment for a final snatch at life for all of them. The door opened and Arlene emerged, wrapped in a brown dress and he barked the question at her.

"You have a pistol?"

"No," she said. "There might be some in the trading post. I know there are rifles there."

Fargo frowned in thought. "He has a clear view from where he is. He'd see me carrying a rifle. But I could hide a pistol. Is there a back way out?"

"No, it's solid all around except for the front doors," Arlene said.

"Shit," Fargo swore. "That kills that idea."

"There's no foundation. Maybe you could dig your way under in the back and crawl in," Arlene suggested.

"I'd need time and we don't have time. If I don't show up with you in another minute or two he'll take off and kill Amanda. He'll figure we're up to something and he'll go after her." He took Arlene's arm and started up the corridor with her. He'd almost reached the front room when he halted. "The kitchen, there has to be a knife in the kitchen," he said.

"Yes, a half dozen," Amanda said and led him into

the wide room with the clay oven and iron stove. She pulled a tray out from beneath a small table and he saw the array of knives. He chose one with a six-inch blade, small enough to hide yet large enough to do its job. He tucked it into the pocket of his jeans and started outside with Arlene. The dawn had started to streak the distant sky when he hurried from the inn with her and walked toward the cluster of black oak where he knew Desmond Kray waited.

Kray came forward when he entered the trees with Arlene. Fargo saw the gun pointed at him as Kray looked down from his horse. "Put your hands up, Fargo," Kray ordered and Fargo obeyed. "Now turn around slow and easy," Kray said and again Fargo obeyed and saw the man's eyes searching for a pistol or a telltale bulge anywhere. "All right, mount up," Kray said, satisfied. "She rides with you."

Fargo climbed onto the Ovaro and pulled Arlene up in the saddle in front of him. He started back again the way they had come and saw Kray fall in directly behind him, his pistol still unwavering. The day came and with it the hot sun and in its glare, no chance to make a move. He'd have to create an opportunity, Fargo realized, and his whisper came between lips that hardly moved. "Tell him you're feeling sick and want to stop," he hissed as they rode through a narrow passage between two boulders.

"Kray . . . can we stop?" Arlene asked, lifting her voice without turning to glance back. "I'm feeling faint."

"No," Kray snapped. "Keep riding."

Fargo cursed inwardly and kept the horse moving slowly as he wondered why Kray was delaying. Perhaps he wanted the pleasure of killing them all together. It was entirely possible. Desmond Kray was the kind of man who'd take an extra measure of twisted satisfaction in that. Fargo put his face against Arlene's cheek. "You're going to faint and fall off the horse. Can you do it?" he asked.

"Yes," she breathed.

"In an hour from now, when I tell you," he said and moved back in the saddle. He cast an eye skyward. The sun had already begun its path downward in the sky. It'd be dusk when they reached Amanda. The dusk would help but Fargo felt his mouth thin. Did he dare wait? Kray could change his mind any moment. But more importantly, he was made of acute cunning. If Arlene fainted after the day began to cool he'd smell a rat instantly. Fargo rode on as he wrestled with his options. He decided to let another hour go by until his own instincts told him to act. He spotted a thick growth of high brush among the oaks and his face came against Arlene's cheek again. "Now," he hissed and drew back.

Arlene waited only a moment and he knew she was gathering herself. "I can't . . . I can't go on," he heard her cry out, her voice quavering, and then she toppled sideways from the saddle. He made a mock grab for her as she fell, hit the ground on her side and rolled onto her back, her eyes closed.

"Goddamn, she's fainted," he snapped as he reined up, glancing at Kray, whose eyes were on Arlene but flicked back to him at once.

"Back away and get off the horse," Kray snapped and Fargo swung to the ground after he moved back a few paces. Kray dismounted but the pistol stayed trained on him. "Stay right where you are," Kray ordered and Fargo shrugged helplessly. Kray knelt down to Arlene, slapped her twice, and saw her head turn limply. Kray's eyes went back to Fargo instantly and he rose, the revolver still trained on Fargo. "Pick her up and lay her over the saddle. You can walk along-side. It's not far, now," the man ordered.

Fargo nodded and went around to the other side of the young woman. He knew this was the moment. There might not be another and he lifted Arlene by her arms, purposely being awkward. She started to sink and he grabbed her around the waist with one arm as he placed himself behind and against her. Kray couldn't see his hand steal into his pocket. "Come on, for Christ's sake," he growled impatiently. Fargo whistled and the Ovaro trotted to him. Keeping the horse between him and Kray, Fargo started to lift Arlene to put her on her stomach across the saddle and his hand tightened around the handle of the knife. It was no perfectly balanced throwing knife but it would have to do. As he lifted Arlene onto the saddle his arm came around in a quick motion still hidden from Kray's sight.

He went the knife through the air and winced at the waviness of its trajectory. Kray's eyes grew wide as he saw the knife. He tried to twist away from it but the blade slammed into his right forearm and Kray cursed in pain as it sliced into him. As he swerved from behind the Ovaro Fargo saw the gun fall from his hand and he charged at the man. Seeing he had no chance to retrieve the fallen gun, Desmond Kray straightened and spun his horse around. Fargo had to dive aside to avoid the animal's hind-quarters slamming into him. He regained his balance and saw Kray racing away and then he remembered. Kray had his Colt in his belt and he was on his way to keep his word.

Arlene had slid from the saddle and was standing behind the Ovaro as Fargo raced for the horse and vaulted onto the saddle, not wasting the precious sec-onds needed to pause and pick up Kray's gun. "Stay here," he yelled back at Arlene as he sent the Ovaro into a full gallop. He could hear Kray's horse ahead of him, also in a full gallop. The narrow, meandering path appeared that led to the pond and Fargo cursed. Kray was halfway down it already. He dug his knees into the Ovaro and the horse responded with that extra burst of power that was his and Fargo caught sight of Kray moments after.

The man heard him closing fast, turned in the saddle, and fired two shots at him, both wide and wild. Fargo flattened himself across the Ovaro's jet-black neck as he charged onward. He could see the path widen and the pond only a thousand yards ahead. He cursed, all the bitterness of defeat in the sound. Kray would reach it first with plenty of time to put a bullet into Amanda without hardly slowing. He'd keep his murdering promise and keep racing on, aware that Fargo would stop to go to Amanda.

Kray disappeared from his sight as the path ended and he swerved to the side where Amanda was bound to the tree and Fargo roared in helpless despair as he raced to the end of the path. But the shot should have sounded by now, he frowned, and he stayed flat against the horse's neck as he reached the end of the path and swerved around to the right. He skidded the horse to a halt as he stared down at Desmond Kray. The man lay on the ground, three arrows deep into his chest. Fargo shot a glance at the tree and saw Amanda still bound to it. As he leaped to the ground the three figures stepped from the shadows, Red Bull in the forefront, his bow still in his hand.

The Cheyenne spoke to him and used his hand to add signs. "We came on her," he said, gesturing to Amanda, who nodded.

"I said Kray's name," she spoke up. "They asked

me something and I didn't understand but I made them know it was Kray who'd tied me here."

Fargo heard the wry grunt escape him. "I'll be damned," he said, returning his eyes to the Cheyenne chief. "You knew he'd come back for her," he said and Red Bull nodded slowly.

"We wait," the Indian said. "We know and we wait. It is always good to wait for revenge." Another Cheyenne came from the trees leading the Indian ponies and the Cheyenne chief pulled himself up on his gray-white pony. He paused to glance at Fargo again. "All done now," he said and made the sign for exchanging. It was a sign common to all sign language and all tribes and it was absolutely clear. You just had to supply the ingredients that were being exchanged— pelts, gifts, wampum, or death.

The Cheyenne faded into the trees and Fargo untied Amanda and she clung to him for a long moment before he pulled her to her feet. He retrieved his Colt and the throwing knife in its calf holster and he paused to stare down at the lifeless form of Desmond Kray.

"He had his gun raised. He was going to shoot me as he rode past when the arrows hit him," Amanda said and shuddered.

"I underestimated him," Fargo said. "But it's finished now. We have to go back and get Arlene."

"Arlene?" Amanda echoed in surprise.

"I'll explain as we ride," he said. She got her army mount and led Kray's horse back with him. The night was deep when they reached the place he'd left Arlene and Fargo saw her step from behind a tree, relief flooding her face. He took Arlene back within sight of the barracks on Kray's horse, Amanda beside him, and let Arlene go on alone while he watched her until she'd dismounted and gone into the inn. He wanted no chance meetings with the lieutenant or Doc Schroder. He'd had enough of explanations. "Let's ride," he said to Amanda as he started back the way they had come.

She nodded eagerly. "And take up where we left off," she said.

"Best damn idea I've heard all day," Fargo agreed.

LOOKING FORWARD!

**The following is the opening
section from the next novel in the exciting
Trailsman series from Signet:**

THE TRAILSMAN #131
BEARTOWN BLOODSHED

*1860—Beartown, where
those who asked too many questions
wound up six feet under . . .*

The trouble started the moment the two lovely women appeared.

Skye Fargo had taken hold of the saddle horn and was about to swing onto his pinto stallion when he spied the pair of blond beauties hurrying down the dusty street in his general direction. The sight of them would have stopped any man in his tracks, not only because both had full figures, long golden tresses, and almost perfect facial features, but because they were identical twins, as alike as two peas in a pod. Every single male in sight was staring at them, but they paid absolutely no attention. They walked side by side, their gazes fixed straight ahead, indicating by their bearing and their walk that they were proper ladies and not fallen doves from any of the many saloons in Beartown. Their demeanor should have discouraged any of the rowdier element from bothering them.

But it didn't.

Fargo saw three men who had been lounging in front of the Lucky Dollar straighten and step farther out into the street, blocking the path of the women. The two lovelies paused. In unison they frowned and went to bypass the men. But the youngest of the trio, a dandy in a fine suit and a wide-brimmed white hat, grabbed the nearest woman by the wrist and held fast. She gave him a look that would have melted a rock, and when he made a comment she tried to pull her arm free to no avail. All three men laughed.

Skye had seen enough. He let go of the saddle horn and walked toward the troublemakers. Oddly, none of the other men lining the street made any move to intervene, and ordinarily Western men wouldn't tolerate seeing a decent woman bothered. He loosened his big Colt in its holster and held his arm loose, ready for action. Neither the women nor the men, who had their backs to him, noticed his approach, and when he was close enough he heard the dandy speaking.

". . . no call to be so unfriendly, Mercia. I just want you to have a drink with me, is all."

"You know darn well, Lucas Cord, that I don't drink," responded the woman whose arm he held. "Now, let me go this instant or else."

"Or else what?" Lucas responded in a mocking tone. "You'll call the marshal?"

The other two men chuckled. Both wore typical frontier clothes and had pistols on their right hips. One was bearded, the other as thin as a rail.

"Leave my sister be!" threw in the second blonde, taking a half step toward Lucas Cord. "There are good men in this town who will hold you to account if you harm us."

"I don't want to harm you," Lucas replied, still holding Mercia's wrist. "All I want is a little company." He lowered his voice. "And as for the good men of Beartown, there isn't a damn one who will lift a finger against me and you know it."

By then Fargo was directly behind the dandy. "Wrong," he said, and seizing Cord by the shoulder he spun him partially around and planted a sweeping right fist on the point of Cord's angular chin. The man tottered backward, releasing Mercia in the process, his arms flailing wildly, and crashed onto his back. For several seconds no one else moved. They all appeared stunned. Then one of the other men, the bearded one, made a grab for the revolver strapped around his waist. Fargo palmed and leveled his Colt before the man could clear leather, and the bearded man froze. "Pull that, mister, and you'll be six feet under by sundown," he warned.

Blinking in disbelief, the bearded man slowly raised his gun hand. "Damn!" he exclaimed. "Never saw anyone that fast before."

Fargo wagged his Colt at the dazed Cord. "Pick up your friend and get out of here. And don't let me catch you bothering these ladies again."

The thin man, who wore a brown shirt, Levi's, and a black hat, cocked his head to study Skye intently. "I don't know who you are, mister, but you're making a big mistake."

"I've made them before," Fargo said, "and I'm still alive. Now do as I told you before you make me lose my temper."

"Let's do as he says, Tillman," the bearded one declared nervously. He moved over to Lucas Cord and hooked his arms under one shoulder. After a moment's hesitation the man called Tillman took the other side, and together they hoisted Cord erect and carted him off into the saloon.

Only then did Skye slip the Colt into his holster and tip his hat to the women. "Ladies," he said politely, and started to turn.

"Hold on!" Mercia exclaimed. "We must thank you for your gallant rescue. Who are you, sir?"

"Skye Fargo."

"I'm Mercia Whitman and this is my sister, Marcia."

Close up, Skye still couldn't tell them apart. They both had striking green eyes and smooth complexions, their rosy mouths were exactly the same shape, and even their noses were identical. He's seen twins before but never two so alike. "Pleased to meet you," he said. "Now, if you'll excuse me," he added, and again went to leave.

"What's your hurry, Mr. Fargo?" Mercia asked, impulsively taking his arm.

"I'm on my way to Fort Laramie to see an old friend," Fargo explained.

"You don't intend to stay the night in Beartown?" Mercia inquired.

"No, ma'am," Skye answered. "I just stopped off to buy a few supplies and wet my whistle." He realized their voices were also identical and wondered how in the world anyone could tell the two apart.

Mercia and Mercia exchanged a strange glance and Mercia nodded.

"Surely you have time for some coffee?" Mercia then said. "Allow us to treat you. It's the least we can do for the service you've rendered."

Skye didn't feel particularly thirsty. But he wasn't about to pass up the chance to enjoy the company of two beautiful women. And since he had plenty of time to reach Fort Laramie, there was no reason to decline the invitation. "All right," he said. "Where to?"

"There's a nice restaurant just down the street," Mercia said.

"Lead the way," Fargo directed, and was pleasantly surprised when the sisters stepped up, one on either side of him, and hooked an arm in the crook of his elbow. They began walking and he fell in step. To a casual bystander it appeared as if he was doing the escorting.

"We'd like you to tell us all about yourself," Mercia commented.

"Oh, yes," Marcia confirmed. "Everything. It isn't often we meet a gentleman of your caliber."

Fargo grinned. He was certain they were up to something, but for the life of him he couldn't figure out what it was. Given the way they had acted toward Lucas Cord, they were being a bit too friendly, a bit too pushy. Not that he minded. He had been on the trail for days and relished this chance to enjoy the company of two such lovely women. Their perfume tingled his nostrils, and he couldn't help but observe how nicely their bosoms filled out the tops of their attractive blue dresses. Which prompted a question. "I should think you ladies would wear different-colored clothes just so folks can tell you apart."

They both giggled.

"We'll tell you a secret," Mercia said. "We like confusing people. Ever since we were babies, no one has been able to tell which one of us was which except for our mother and father—" She broke off, sadness lining her face. Then she took a breath and continued. "It's been great fun. When we were younger we would change seats in school, and our poor teacher would never know the difference."

"And we would pretend to be the other one at family gatherings, and our relatives would never be the wiser," Marcia mentioned.

"How do your parents tell who is who?" Fargo idly asked.

"Our mother is dead," Mercia said softly. "She died on the way out here, over a year ago. Came down with a high fever one day after a rain and she never recovered. We didn't have a doctor on the wagon train, so there was little we could do."

"Sorry to hear it," Fargo sympathized, and opted to change the subject. "How about your father? How does he tell who is who?"

"We'll talk about him later," Mercia said.

"There's the restaurant," Marcia declared, pointing at an establishment bearing a large sign that read "RUTH'S FINE EATS." "Wait until you meet Ruth. She's the kindest person in this whole town."

Skye let himself be led to the double doors. Had he detected a trace of anger in Marcia's tone when she referred to the town, or had it been his imagination? He opened a door for the sisters, then entered a spacious room containing four long tables lined with chairs. Red tablecloths and pink curtains gave the place a homey atmosphere, as did the delicious aroma of cooking food that wafted through an open door at the back of the room, through which the kitchen could be glimpsed. Only two other customers were there, an elderly couple in a corner.

Mercia moved to a table on the opposite side of the room and halted behind a chair.

"Allow me," Fargo said, and seated both of them

before sitting with his back to the wall so he could keep an eye on the entrance. For all he knew, Lucas Cord might want revenge.

A white-haired matron in a lavender dress and a white apron came out of the kitchen, caught sight of them, and beamed as she walked on over. "Marcia and Mercia! How delightful. You girls haven't been to see me in days."

"Hello, Ruth," Marcia responded. "We'd like some of your wonderful coffee."

"Sorry about not visiting you," Mercia said, frowning. "But we've been too upset to go anywhere."

Ruth halted and nodded. "I understand, dearie." She glanced at Skye, examining him as she might an insect that had the temerity to trespass in her kitchen. "And who is this, might I ask?"

"His name is Skye Fargo," Mercia disclosed. "He just stopped Lucas Cord from giving us a bad time."

At the mention of Cord's name the matron's brown eyes narrowed. "Again?" she said absently, and wiped her thick hands on her apron. "When will that boy learn?"

"Lucas is no boy," Marcia said. "He's a lecher who thinks every woman should swoon at his feet when he smiled at them. One of these days he'll go too far and someone will put a bullet in his brain."

"For two cents I'd do it," Ruth said, and motioned at Marcia. "Why don't you join me in the kitchen for a minute? You can help me carry back the pot and the cups."

"Certainly," Marcia replied.

Fargo watched them stroll off, then focused on Mercia, searching for a blemish, a mole perhaps, or a tiny childhood scar that would enable him to tell the sisters apart. She steadily returned his stare and grinned.

"You're wasting your time, I assure you."

"Can you read thoughts?" Fargo joked.

"Experience, Mr. Fargo."

"Call me Skye," he said, and happened to turn toward the elderly couple in the corner. They were regarding him with the oddest expressions, and they immediately averted their gazes and forked roast beef into their mouths. Now, what was that all about? he asked himself.

"Would you happen to be in need of money, Skye?" Mercia unexpectedly inquired.

Fargo looked at her. "The coffee will be thanks enough."

"I'm not offering to pay you for having helped us," Mercia said. "My sister and I are thinking of hiring you for a job we can't do ourselves."

"Oh? When did you decide this? I don't recollect the two of you talking about it on the way to the restaurant."

"We didn't have to discuss it," Mercia said. "This might seem bizarre to you, but frequently we know what the other is thinking without having to say a word. We've been this way since we were little girls. I can still recall the very first time it happened," she paused. "We were at the supper table and I wanted the butter. It was on the other side of Marcia, and before I could open my mouth to ask for it, she handed the dish to me. I don't know what to call this talent, but it definitely exists. Marcia and I are living proof."

"So you do read thoughts," Skye said, smiling.

"Maybe the two of you should sign up with a traveling show. You could make good money."

Mercia laughed. "No, thanks. I don't want to be considered a freak of nature. My sister and I don't advertise our talent. It's strictly between us, and even then we don't always see eye to eye. Although we're practically identical physically, there are certain differences between us. Her personality is nothing like mine. She seldom loses her composure while I am very emotional."

Fargo was about to remark that he liked emotional women when the double doors slammed open and in strode an enraged Lucas Cord, a smirking Tillman, and the guy with the beard. Cord glared about until he spied Fargo, then he squared his shoulders and stalked forward. An ivory-handled Colt was thrust in the waistband of his pants, and his right hand hovered near it like talons of a bird of prey about to swoop down on a rabbit.

"You!" Cord bellowed. "On your feet! I don't like to kill a man who doesn't have a fair break."

Skye sighed and pushed his chair back from the table. For a man who didn't go out of his way to seek trouble, he certainly found more than his share. He had no desire to gun down this dandy who acted about ten sizes too big for his britches, but he wasn't about to back down, either. "You don't know when to leave well enough alone, Cord."

Lucas stopped, his body rigid. "You struck me, you son of a bitch! Now stand up and take your medicine."

Whether it was Cord's insolent tone or the fact these men were prodding him when all he wanted was to be left alone, Fargo couldn't say. But suddenly something snapped deep inside of him, and he came out of his chair so swiftly that Lucas Cord involuntarily took a step backward and Tillman lost his arrogant smirk. Instead of drawing, Fargo walked straight toward them. The guy with the beard looked as if he desperately wanted to be somewhere else. Tillman seemed startled. And Cord's right hand trembled above the gun.

"That's close enough!" Lucas cried, extending his left hand, palm out. "Stop right there."

Skye had no intention of stopping. He advanced until he was mere inches from Cord and snapped, "Go ahead. Die if you want to."

Lucas Cord gulped. His face became a bright shade of crimson. He clenched and unclenched his right hand, then abruptly moved a pace backward and crouched like a cougar about to pounce. "You don't know who you're dealing with, mister," he growled. "I'm the son of Rory Cord."

"So?"

Surprise etched Cord's face. "Rory Cord, owner of the RC ranch," he elaborated in a tone that implied his father was a man to be reckoned with.

"Never heard of it."

"Everyone has heard of my father," Lucas said in disbelief, then added smugly. "He's the biggest man in these parts. And when you tangle with me, you tangle with him."

Contempt welled up in Fargo. Here was a grown man of twenty or so hiding behind his father's shirttail. Lucas expected him to be intimidated by the news and back down. Unfortunately, he was sadly mistaken. "This is between you and me," he stated flatly. "Your father isn't the one who bothered these women. You did. And now you have the gall to march in here and threaten me. Boy, you're as dumb as they come."

"I'm no boy!" Lucas bristled, and without warning he lunged, swinging both fists at Sky's head.

Taken unawares, Fargo was rocked by a right to the jaw. Back-pedaling, he brought his arms up to protect his face and stomach and warded off several wild punches. Cord seemed to have forgotten all about the gun in his waistband in his mad fury to smash Skye to a pulp. But reckless rage was a poor substitute for seasoned skill, and Fargo had lived through more fights and wild brawls than most ten men. He blocked a blow to the abdomen, then landed a looping right full on Cord's mouth, smashing his lips and sending the dandy staggering into a table. Before he could recover, Fargo closed in. He rammed his knuckles into Cord's mouth again as he tried to straighten, then delivered a flurry that battered him to his knees. Nearly senseless, Cord swayed. Fargo set himself for one final blow when a sharp cry of warning from Mercia rent the air.

"Skye! Behind you!"

Fargo whirled to behold Tillman armed with a dagger just as the thin man sprang. . . .

CANYON O'GRADY RIDES ON

27 million Americans can't read a bedtime story to a child.

It's because 27 million adults in this country simply can't read.

Functional illiteracy has reached one out of five Americans. It robs them of even the simplest of human pleasures, like reading a fairy tale to a child.

You can change all this by joining the fight against illiteracy.

Call the Coalition for Literacy at toll-free **1-800-228-8813** and volunteer.

Volunteer Against Illiteracy. The only degree you need is a degree of caring.